The Larousse Book of

FAIRY TALES

Little Red Riding Hood
goes to see her
Grandmother

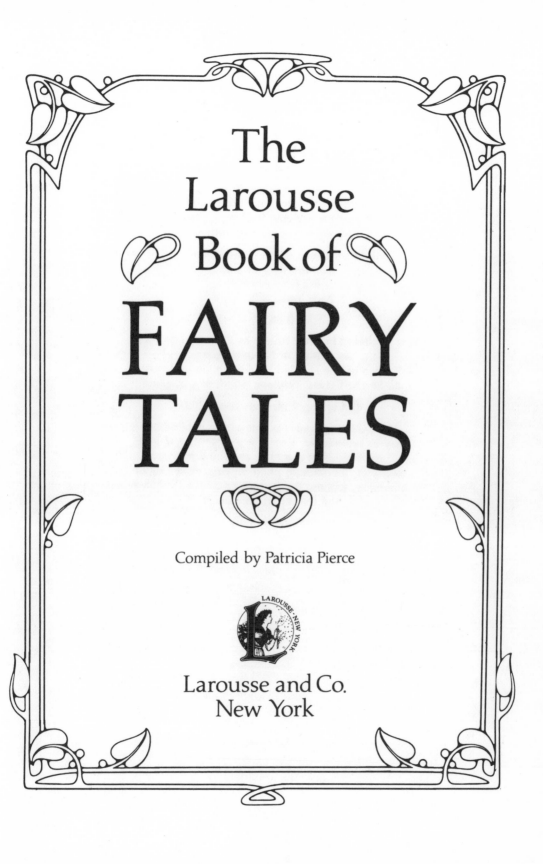

The Larousse Book of FAIRY TALES

Compiled by Patricia Pierce

Larousse and Co.
New York

Frontispiece

Little Red Riding-Hood.
Little Red Riding Hood started off
at once for her grandmother's cottage,
which was in another village.

First published in the United States by
Larousse and Co., Inc.,
572 Fifth Avenue,
New York, N.Y. 10036

ISBN 0-88332-468-7

First published in Great Britain by Country Life Books,
an imprint of Newnes Books,
a division of The Hamlyn Publishing Group Limited,
84-88 The Centre, Feltham, Middlesex, England

Printed in Italy

Contents

Introduction

This book of fairy tales contains a selection of the most popular tales, stories and fables which have come down to us over the centuries. Their vitality testifies to the affection with which they are regarded by both children and adults alike.

This book is illustrated with photographs of turn-of-the-century fairy-tale tile pictures, which appear here for the first time in book form. The fairy tales themselves have been selected from sources of the same period to complement the tile pictures.

The Fairy Tales

The deep well of stories involving fantasy is much older than the written word. Some fairy tales, 'Cinderella' for example, are thought to be at least 1,000 years old. Likely sources for many others can be traced to Eastern folk tales of a similar age.

Fairy tales as we know them first appeared in written form in Venice in 1550 to 1553, when Gianfrancesco Straparola published his collection, *La piace voli Notti* (The Delightful Night). This was followed by another important Italian collection *Lo Cunto de li Cunti* (The Tales of Tales) by Giambattista Basile which was published in three volumes from 1634 to 1636.

Then came the most famous collection, that of Charles Perrault, whose fairy tales were published in France in 1697 under the title *Histoire ou Contes du temps passé. Avec des Moralitez.*

The Babes in the Wood *opposite*: Then the birds collected the leaves, one by one, and gently placed them on the sleeping children.

6

The babes
in the wood.

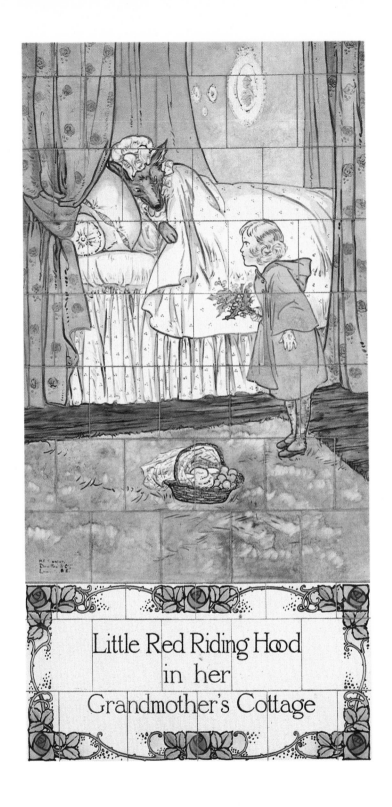

Little Red Riding Hood
in her
Grandmother's Cottage

The collections of Madame d'Aulnoy and Madame de Beaumont followed. From Charles Perrault's collection came the Western versions of 'Cinderella', 'The Sleeping Beauty', 'Puss in Boots' and 'Little Red Riding-Hood', stories included here.

One of the most famous collections was made by Jacob and Wilhelm Grimm in 1812, and 'Hansel and Gretel' is from their book, as is 'The Golden Goose'. Hans Christian Andersen, another great writer of fairy-tales, found his own life transformed, fairy-tale like, from that of poverty to that of fame, because of this. 'The Princess and the Pea', 'The Tinder Box' and 'Thumbelina' were originally from his writings. 'The Story of the Three Bears' was first collected and published by Robert Southey in 1837. 'The Three Little Pigs' was probably Italian.

Some of the fairy tales in this book are traditional English ones, such as 'Dick Whittington', 'Jack and the Beanstalk', 'Henny Penny' and 'Jack the Giant-Killer'. 'Little Goody Two-Shoes', is a favourite nursery story, and is similar to 'The Babes in the Wood', for both are based on real events.

But most, if not all, of the stories, even those written by a known author, have very similar antecedents. Whether they came from the same source, or whether the human imagination evolved in the same way around the world, we can never know. One thing is clear – the love of children and adults for these tales of enchantment. A moralizing theme was usually a later addition. The enduring appeal is the sense of fantasy and wonder.

The Sleeping Beauty pages 8–9: All the fairies who could be found in the kingdom were invited to the christening as godmothers of the little princess.

Little Red Riding-Hood opposite: She went over to the bed; she was surprised to see how strange her grandmother looked in her nightcap.

Through these tales we first experience humour, romance, adventure and terror. The forces of good and of evil are depicted in strong, clear colours. Justice usually prevails. The impossible happens – animals talk and take part in the fantastical happenings; giants and dwarfs appear regularly – as does, occasionally, even a fairy godmother.

The Tile Pictures

The fairy-tale tile pictures were made by Doulton between 1890 and the First World War. They were used to decorate the children's wards of hospitals in Britain and the Empire, of which there was a building boom around the turn of the century. The tiles were beautifully hand-painted by leading artists.

Sometimes a donor sponsored the tiles for a whole ward, with a tile picture of a fairy-tale or a nursery-rhyme character above each little bed. (A poster still exists, showing just such a children's ward at St. Thomas' Hospital, London. See page 172.) The rest of the ward might be covered with plain tiles and a suitable tile plaque acknowledging the donor. More often, each tile picture was donated by an individual or an organisation. As well as being colourful, decorative and entertaining, the tiles were useful because they were easy to clean and therefore hygienic. The surviving tile pictures, usually in remarkably good condition, are a tribute to the skill of the Victorian tile makers.

Tile pictures of fairy tales and nursery rhymes, made by Doulton and other companies, still exist in at least sixty hospitals, mainly in Britain, but also in Wellington, New Zealand and Poona, India. The same subjects often appear in different hospitals. Because they were hand-painted, no two tile pictures of the same subject are exactly alike.

Additional illustrations have been included here with this Introduction to enable us to introduce more tile pictures of some of the stories – 'The Babes in the Wood', 'The Sleeping Beauty', 'Little Red Riding-Hood' and 'Cinderella', as well as to show the variety of styles used to depict the same subject.

The Artists

Doulton's reputation as manufacturers of all types of decorative tiling at the turn of the century was unrivalled. In 1904 the company published a catalogue of their pictorial tiles entitled *Pictures in Pottery* and this led to numerous commissions for tile panels in children's wards. The main artists seem to have been M.E. Thompson, William Rowe and John H. McLennan. Some were signed only 'Doulton, Lambeth' or not signed at all, so we may never know for certain who the artist was.

Margaret Thompson worked for Doulton & Co., from *c.* 1889 to *c.* 1926. She specialised in designing murals depicting legends, nursery rhymes and fairy tales. Her tile pictures are signed: 'M.E. Thompson, Doulton & Co. Ltd., Lambeth S.E.' A talented artist, she also designed faience vases and bowls for Doulton & Co., and illustrated children's books. Her fairy-tale tile pictures have a charm that is unsurpassed in work of this kind. Simply and beautifully, Margaret Thompson captured the essence of these well-loved fairy-tale characters. Willam Rowe was a designer and decorator at Doulton & Co. from 1882 to 1939. A very able etcher and painter of water colours, he exhibited at the Royal Academy. Tile-painting was his main field, his major work being six panels, 23 feet by 62 feet, for the Booking Hall at Singapore Terminal Station. His tile pictures are signed simply 'W.R.'

John H. McLennan, who often seems to have worked in conjunction with William Rowe on tile panels, worked for Doulton & Co. from 1879 to 1910. He was a designer and painter of faience vases, plaques, wall tiles and mural panels. Hand-painted pictorial tile panels were his speciality, and they were signed with his initials: 'W.H.McL.' John McLennan's work won acclaim at many international exhibitions, and he secured commissions from the King of Siam and the Czar of Russia. From today's point in time, such commissions – from exotic personages who lived in great splendour in faraway places – somehow seem fitting for an artist who so ably depicted the fantasy world of fairy tales.

In time, tile pictures became unfashionable, and many were destroyed, given away, or covered up. More recently, they have once again been appreciated as works of art in their own right. Often when an old hospital is being replaced by a new one, efforts are renewed to preserve, restore and re-site the tile pictures so they can be enjoyed by all. In carrying out our research, we have, in some cases, been able to put the Administration of a hospital interested in preserving their tile pictures in touch with a hospital that has already accomplished this.

Some tile pictures still remain hidden, but intact, under layers of paint, or behind partitions and medicine shelves, waiting for the day when they will once again be revealed to entertain 'the young invalides' and everyone who passes by.   P.P.

Cinderella *opposite*: When her work was done, which happened sometimes, she would sit in the chimney corner, dreaming of things which no one knows.

Cinderella *page 16*: She became aware of a blue mist gathering and revolving upon itself. It spun itself to a standstill and there was the strangest little lady you could ever imagine.

Cinderella
in the
Chimney Corner.

Cinderella and her
Fairy Godmother

The
FAIRY
TALES

The Tinder-Box

soldier went marching along the road. 'Left, right, left, right!' He had his knapsack on his back, and a sabre at his side, for he was coming home from the war.

On the high road he met an old witch; she was very repulsive to look at: her under lip hung down over her chin. 'Good evening, soldier,' she said. 'What a fine sabre you have got! And what a large knapsack! You are something like a soldier, and you shall have as much money as ever you like.'

'Thank you, old witch,' said the soldier.

'Do you see that tall tree yonder?' said the witch. 'It is hollow inside. Climb up to the top and you will see a hole through which you can let yourself down right into the tree. I will tie a rope round you so that I can pull you up again when you call to me.'

'What am I to do when I am down the tree?' asked the soldier.

'Fetch up money,' said the witch. 'Below the roots of the tree you will find a large hall, lighted up with more than three hundred lamps. Then you will see three doors; open them all, the key is in each lock. In the first room you will see a large chest in the middle of the floor, and on the chest a dog with eyes as big as saucers. Don't mind him in the least. Here is my blue-checked apron; spread that out on the floor and put the dog upon it, then open the chest and take out as much copper as you like. If you prefer silver you must go on into the next room. But *there* is a dog with eyes as big as mill-wheels – you need not fear him, however. Put him on my apron and take out the money. If you want gold, you can have it, as much as ever you can carry, by going into the third room; but the dog on the chest of gold has eyes as big as steeples – he is a savage brute, you may take my word for it. Never fear him, however; put him on my apron; he won't hurt you, and you can take as much gold as you will.'

'That doesn't sound amiss,' said the soldier. 'But what am I to give you for it, old witch? For I don't suppose you mean to do it for nothing.'

'I do,' said the witch. 'I won't take a penny. All I ask is that you shall bring me up an old tinder-box that my grandmother left behind her the last time she was there.'

'Well, then,' said the soldier, 'tie the rope round my waist.'

'Here it is,' said the witch, 'and here is my blue-checked apron.'

The soldier climbed up the tree, let himself down, and stood, as the witch had said, in a great hall where hundreds of lamps were burning. He opened the first door. Ugh! There sat the dog with eyes as big as saucers, glaring at him. 'You're a nice fellow!' said the soldier, lifting him on to the witch's apron.

Then he filled his pockets with copper, shut the chest, and went into the next room. Right enough, there sat the dog with eyes as big as mill-wheels.

'You had better not stare so,' said the soldier; 'your eyes might come out of your head altogether.' He lifted the dog on to the witch's apron, and at the sight of all the silver in the chest, he emptied his pockets again, and filled them and his knapsack too with silver. Then he went into the third room. That really was awful! The dog had eyes every inch as big as steeples, and they both spun round like wheels.

'I hope you are well,' said the soldier, saluting, for he had never seen a dog like that before. But when he had looked at him long enough he thought, 'Well, I must be quick.' He lifted him on to the apron and opened the chest. Heavens! What a heap of gold! Enough to buy up all the town: all the barley sugar, tin soldiers, whips and rocking-horses in the whole world. The soldier soon threw away all the silver, and filled his pockets, knapsack, cap, and even his boots with gold. He could hardly walk, but he had the money. He put the dog back on the chest, shut the door and called up the tree. 'Now pull me up, old witch.'

'Have you got the tinder-box?' asked the witch.

'Heart alive!' said the soldier, 'I quite forgot that.'

He went back and fetched it; the witch pulled him up, and there he stood on the high road, with his pockets, knapsack, cap, and boots brimful of gold.

'What do you want with the tinder-box?' asked the soldier.

'That's no business of yours,' said the witch; 'you have your money; give me the box.'

'What's that you say?' cried the soldier. 'Tell me this very minute what you want it for, or I'll draw my sword and cut off your head.'

'I won't!' said the witch.

The soldier immediately cut off her head. There she lay. He tied up all his money in her apron, slung it like a bundle over his shoulder, put the tinder-box in his pocket, and walked on towards the town.

It was a splendid town. The soldier went into one of the best hotels, engaged the largest room, and ordered everything he liked best for supper. He was rich now, because he had so much money.

The man who blacked his boots thought it was strange that such a rich gentleman should wear such very old boots, but the next day the soldier bought new ones, and a new suit of clothes. He was not a soldier now, but a fine gentleman; and the people spoke to him of all the remarkable things in the town, of the king, and the beautiful young princess, his daughter.

'Where can one see her?' asked the soldier.

'You cannot see her,' was the reply; 'she lives in a large brazen castle, surrounded by walls and turrets. No one but the king may enter, because it was once prophesied that she would marry a common soldier.'

'I should like to look at her,' said the soldier; but it was quite impossible for him to obtain permission.

From this time he lived a merry life, going to theatres, and driving about in the royal parks and gardens. He gave away a great deal to the poor, and that was right of him: he knew of old what it is not to have a shilling in one's pocket. Now he was rich, wore fine clothes, and had numbers of friends, who all said he was an excellent fellow and a perfect gentleman. The soldier was pleased at that. But unluckily, as he went on spending money every day, and never earning any more, he found himself at last with scarcely any left, and was obliged to leave his beautiful rooms for a little garret under the roof, where he had to black his own boots, and mend them with a packing-needle. None of his friends came to see him now – there were too many steps to climb.

It was a dark night, and he could not even buy himself a

candle; but it suddenly occurred to him that there was a piece of candle left in the tinder-box which he had fetched up for the old witch, out of the hollow tree. He struck a light, and the moment it flashed up, the door opened, and in came the dog with eyes as big as saucers.

'What does my lord require?' said the dog.

'What is this?' said the soldier. 'This is a lively sort of a tinder-box if I can get whatever I like out of it! Get me some money,' he said to the dog, and *whish*! off he went – *whish*! there he was back again with a bag full of copper in his mouth.

Then the soldier began to see what a wonderful box it was. You struck it once, and up came the dog with eyes as big as saucers; you struck it twice, and up came the one that sat on the chest of silver; three times, and up came the one that kept guard over the gold. The soldier moved downstairs again into his beautiful rooms, and bought some more fine clothes. Then all his friends knew him again at once, and thought a great deal of him.

One day he began to think how extraordinary it was that nobody could get to see the princess. Every one said she was very beautiful, but what was the good of that if she had to live in a brazen castle surrounded by high walls? 'Can't I manage to see her?' he thought. 'Where is my tinder-box?' He struck a light and up came the dog with eyes as big as saucers. 'I know it is the middle of the night,' said the soldier; 'but I should like to look at the princess for a minute or so.'

The dog was out of the house in a second, and before the soldier could draw breath, *whish*! there he was back again, with the princess on his back. She lay there fast asleep; so beautiful that anyone could see she was a princess. The soldier could not help kissing her once, very soldier-like.

Then the dog ran back with the princess. But the next morning when the king and queen were at breakfast, the princess said that she had had a very strange dream in the night; she had ridden along on a dog's back, and been kissed by a soldier.

'That's a pretty story!' said the queen.

The next night one of the old ladies-in-waiting was ordered to watch by the princess's bed, and see whether it was really a dream, or what was the meaning of it.

The soldier felt a great longing to see the princess again, so the dog was sent to fetch her, and ran for her as quickly as before. But the lady-in-waiting was awake; she put on galoshes and ran behind them, and when she saw the dog disappear in a large house, she put a cross on the door with a piece of chalk. Then she went home and got into bed, and the dog came back with the princess. But when he saw a cross on the house where the soldier lived, *he* took a piece of chalk and put a cross on every house in the town. That was rather clever on his part, because now the lady-in-waiting could not possibly tell which was the right door.

Early the next morning, down came the king and queen, with the lady-in-waiting and all the army, to see where the princess had been.

'There it is!' cried the king, as soon as he saw the first cross on a door.

'No, there it is, my dear husband,' said the queen, looking at the second cross.

'But *there's* one and *there's* one!' cried everybody at once; for wherever they looked nothing was to be seen but crosses. Then they understood that it was of no use looking any farther.

Now the queen was a very clever woman, who could do more than ride in a carriage. She took out her golden scissors, cut up a piece of silk, and made it into a pretty little bag. She then filled it with flour, and tied it round the princess's waist, so that the flour might be strewn all along the way she went.

That night the dog came again, and carried off the princess; the soldier had now fallen deeply in love with her, and would gladly have married her.

The dog never noticed the flour as it fell all along the road from the castle to the soldier's room. The next morning the king and queen saw clearly where their daughter had been, and the soldier was immediately arrested, and put in prison.

There he had to stop. It was dull and gloomy enough, and all they said to him was, 'You will be hanged tomorrow!' *That* was not exactly cheering, and his tinder-box was left behind in his lodgings. The next morning, as he looked through the iron bars of his window, he saw the crowds of people hurrying into the town to see him hanged. He heard the drums beating, and saw the soldiers marching by. Everybody was out, even a shoemaker's lad, in his apron and slippers, who was running so fast that one of his slippers fell off, and flew right up against the window where the soldier stood.

'Hallo! my lad,' cried the soldier; 'you need not be in such a tremendous hurry; they won't begin without me. If you would like to earn some money, just run to my lodgings, and fetch me my tinder-box; you shall have a shilling for your trouble, but you must be quick about it.'

The lad thought he should like to earn the shilling, so he fetched the tinder-box, gave it to the soldier, and – well, now we shall hear.

The gallows was set up outside the town, and round it stood the soldiers and thousands of people. The king and queen sat on a splendid throne, opposite the judges and council. The soldier mounted the ladder, the rope was placed round his neck, when he said that the last harmless wish of a poor wretch was always granted, and he begged permission to smoke a pipe of tobacco – it would be his last pipe in the world.

The king granted his request, and the soldier struck his box – once, twice, thrice! In a moment, up sprang the three dogs – the one with eyes as big as saucers – the one with eyes as big as mill-wheels – and the one with eyes as big as steeples.

'Help me, so that I shall not be hanged,' said the soldier. And the dogs flew at the judges and at all the council, seizing one by the leg and one by the nose, and tossing them up in the air to such a height that they fell down, and broke all to bits.

'I won't be tossed!' said the king, but up he went, and the queen after him. That frightened the soldiers and the people to such a degree, that they cried out 'Noble soldier! You shall be our king, and marry the princess.'

Then they handed the soldier into the king's carriage, and the three dogs ran by the side and cried, 'Hurrah!' The street boys whistled through their fingers, and the soldiers presented arms. The princess was set free from the brazen castle, and became queen, which pleased her exceedingly. The wedding festivities lasted eight days, and the dogs sat up to table and stared with all their might.

Puss in Boots

A miller who was dying divided all his property between his three children. This was a very simple matter, as he had nothing to leave but his mill, his ass, and his cat; so he made no will, and called in no lawyer, for he would probably have taken a large slice out of these poor possessions. The eldest son took the mill, the second the ass, while the third was obliged to content himself with the cat, at which he grumbled very much.

'My brothers,' said he, 'by putting their property together may gain an honest livelihood, but there is nothing left for me except to die of hunger; unless, indeed, I were to kill my cat and eat him, and make a coat out of his skin, which would be very scanty clothing.'

The cat, who heard the young man talking to himself, looked at him with a grave and wise air, and said, 'Master, I think you had better not kill me. I shall be much more useful to you alive.'

'How so?' asked his master.

'You have but to give me a sack and a pair of boots such as gentlemen wear when they go shooting, and you will find you are not so ill off as you suppose.'

Now, though the young miller did not put much faith in the cat's words, he thought it rather surprising that a cat should speak at all. And he had before now seen him show so much cleverness in catching rats and mice that it seemed well to trust him a little further, especially as, poor young fellow, there was no one else in the whole wide would for him to trust.

When the cat got his boots he drew them on with a grand air. Then, slinging his sack over his shoulder and drawing the cords of it round his neck, he marched bravely to a rabbit-warren near by, with which he was well acquainted. Putting some bran and lettuces into his bag, and stretching himself out beside it as if he were dead, he waited for some fine, fat young rabbit to peer into the sack to eat the food that was inside. This happened very shortly, for there are plenty of foolish young rabbits in every warren; and when one of them, who really was a splendid fat fellow, put his head inside, Master Puss drew the cords immediately, and took him and killed him without mercy.

Then, very proud of his prey, he marched direct up to the palace, and begged to speak with the King. He was desired to ascend to the apartment of His Majesty, where, making a low bow, he said, 'Sire, here is a magnificent rabbit from the warren of my lord the Marquis of Carabas, which he has desired me to offer humbly to Your Majesty.'

'Tell your master,' replied the King, 'that I accept his present, and am very much obliged to him.'

Another time Puss went and hid himself and his sack in a wheat-field, and there caught two spendid fat partridges in the same manner as he had done the rabbit. When he presented them to the King, with a similar message as before, His Majesty was so pleased that he ordered the cat to be taken down into the kitchen and given something to eat and drink.

One day, hearing that the King was intending to take a drive by the river with his daughter, the most beautiful princess in the world, Puss said to his master, 'Sir, if you would only follow my advice your fortune is made. You have only to go and bathe in the river at a place which I shall show you, and leave all the rest to me. Only remember that you are no longer yourself, but my lord the Marquis of Carabas.'

The miller's son agreed, not that he had any faith in the cat's promise, but because he no longer cared what happened.

While he was bathing the King and all the Court passed by, and were startled to hear loud cries of 'Help! Help! My lord the Marquis of Carabas is drowning!'

The King put his head out of the carriage, and saw nobody but the cat who had at different times brought him so many presents of game; however, he ordered his guards to go quickly to the help of my lord the Marquis of Carabas.

While they were pulling the unfortunate marquis out of the water the cat came up bowing to the side of the King's carriage, and told a long and pitiful story about some thieves, who, while his master was bathing, had come and carried away all his clothes, so that it would be impossible for him to appear before His Majesty and the illustrious princess.

'Oh, we will soon remedy that,' answered the King kindly, and immediately ordered one of the first officers of the household to ride back to the palace with all speed and bring back the most elegant supply of clothes for the young gentleman, who kept in the background until they arrived. Then, being handsome and well made, his new clothes became him so well that he looked as if he had been a marquis all his days, and advanced with an air of respectful ease to offer his thanks to His Majesty.

The King received him courteously, and the princess admired him very much. Indeed, so charming did he appear to her that she persuaded her father to invite him into the carriage with them, which, you may be sure, the young man did not refuse.

The cat, delighted at the success of his scheme, went away as fast as he could, and ran so swiftly that he kept a long way ahead of the royal carriage. He went on and on till he came to some peasants who were mowing in a meadow. 'Good people,' said he, in a very firm voice, 'the King is coming past here shortly, and if you do not say that the field you are mowing belongs to my lord the Marquis of Carabas you shall all be chopped as small as mincemeat.'

So when the King drove by and asked whose meadow it was where there was such a splendid crop of hay, the mowers all answered in trembling tones that it belonged to my lord the Marquis of Carabas.

'You have very fine land, marquis,' said His Majesty to the miller's son.

'Yes, sire,' he answered. 'It is not a bad meadow, take it altogether.'

Then the cat came to a wheat-field, where the reapers were reaping with all their might. He bounced in upon them: 'The King is coming past today, and if you do not tell him that this wheat belongs to my lord the Marquis of Carabas I will have you every one chopped as small as mincemeat.'

The reapers, very much alarmed, did as they were told, and the King congratulated the marquis upon possessing such beautiful fields, laden with such an abundant harvest.

They drove on, the cat always running before and saying the same thing to everybody he met – that they were to declare the whole country belonged to his master; so that even the King was astonished at the vast estate of my lord the Marquis of Carabas.

But now the cat arrived at a great castle where dwelt an ogre, to whom belonged all the land through which the King had been passing. He was a cruel tyrant, and his tenants and servants were terribly afraid of him. This accounted for their being so ready to say whatever they were told to say by the cat, who had taken pains to find out all about the ogre.

So, putting on the boldest face he could assume, Puss marched up to the castle with his boots on, and asked to see the owner of it, saying that he was on his travels, but did not wish to pass so near the castle of such a noble gentleman without paying his respects to him. When the ogre heard this message he went to the door, received the cat as civilly as an ogre can, and begged him to walk in and repose himself.

'Thank you, sir,' said the cat; 'but first I hope you will satisfy a traveller's curiosity. I have heard in far countries of your many remarkable qualities, and especially how you have the power to change yourself into any sort of beast you choose – a lion, for instance, or an elephant.'

'That is quite true,' replied the ogre. 'And lest you should doubt it I will immediately become a lion.'

He did so; and the cat was so frightened that he sprang up to the roof of the castle and hid himself in the gutter – a proceeding rather inconvenient on account of his boots, which were not exactly suitable for walking upon tiles. At length, perceiving that the ogre had resumed his original form, he came down again stealthily, and confessed that he had been very much frightened.

'But, sir,' said he, 'it may be easy enough for such a big gentleman as you to change himself into a large animal; I do not suppose you can become a small one – a rat or mouse, for instance. I have heard that you can; still, for my part, I consider it quite impossible.'

'Impossible?' cried the other indignantly. 'You shall see!' And immediately the cat saw the ogre no longer, but a little mouse running along on the floor.

This was exactly what he wanted; and he did the most natural thing a cat could do in the circumstances – he sprang upon the mouse and gobbled it up in a trice. So there was an end of the ogre.

By this time the King had arrived opposite the castle, and was seized with a strong desire to enter it. The cat, hearing the noise of the carriage-wheels, ran forward in a great hurry, and, standing at the gate, said in a loud voice, 'Welcome, sire, to the castle of my lord the Marquis of Carabas.'

'What!' cried His Majesty, very much surprised, 'Does the castle also belong to you? Truly, marquis, you have kept your secret well up to the last minute. I have never seen anything finer than this courtyard and these battlements. Indeed, I have nothing like them in the whole of my dominions.'

The marquis, without speaking, helped the princess to descend, and, standing aside, that the King might enter first – for he had already acquired all the manners of the Court – followed His Majesty to the great hall, where a magnificent collation had been spread for the ogre and some of his friends. Without more delay they all sat down to feast.

The King, charmed with the good qualities of the Marquis of Carabas – and likewise his wine, of which he had drunk six or

Puss in Boots *opposite*: Master Puss ascended to the apartments of His Majesty, and said 'Sire, here is a magnificent rabbit from the warren of my lord the Marquis of Carabas.'

seven cups – said, bowing across the table at which the princess and the miller's son were talking very confidentially together, 'It rests with you, marquis, whether you will not become my son-in-law.'

'I shall be only too happy,' said the Marquis, very readily, and the princess's eyes declared the same.

So they were married the very next day, and took possession of the ogre's castle, and of everything that had belonged to him.

As for the cat, he became at once a grand personage, and had never more any need to run after mice, except for his own amusement.

Puss in Boots *opposite*: While he was bathing, the King and all the Court passed by and were startled to hear loud cries of 'Help! Help! My lord the Marquis of Carabas is drowning!'

The Sleeping Beauty

nce upon a time there lived a king and queen who were in great trouble because they had no children. They were sorrier about it than words can tell. They offered up prayers, made vows and pilgrimages, moved heaven and earth – and for a long time it all seemed to be of no use.

At last, however, their wish was granted, and the queen became the mother of a baby girl. Such a fine christening was never seen before. All the fairies who could be found in the kingdom – there were seven of them – were invited as godmothers of the little princess. As each one was bound to bring a fairy-gift – this being the custom with the fairies of those times – it stood to reason that the princess would have everything you could think of to make her perfectly good and beautiful and happy.

After the christening was over, the whole company went back to the king's palace, where there was a great festival in honour of the fairies. A magnificent banquet was spread for them, and in front of each fairy was set a box of solid gold, holding a knife and fork and spoon of beaten gold, studded with diamonds and rubies. But, as they all took their places at the table, along came an old fairy who had not been asked to the feast, because for the last fifty years she had never come out of the tower in which she lived, and everybody believed her either dead or under some spell.

The king ordered that a place should be laid for her; but there was no means of giving her a solid gold box like those that had been put before the others, because only seven had been made for the seven fairies who were expected. The old crone thought she had been insulted, and muttered some threat or other between her teeth. Now, one of the young fairies, who happened to be near, heard this. Guessing that the old fairy might revenge herself by bestowing on the little princess some piece of ill-luck, she hid herself behind the tapestries as soon as the company had risen from the table. She did this so that she might be the last to speak, and could repair as far as possible any evil that the old fairy might be intending.

Meanwhile the fairies began to bestow their gifts upon the princess. The youngest promised, as her gift, that the princess should be the most beautiful woman in the world; the next, that she should be cleverer than any mere mortal could hope to be; the third, that whatever she should set her hand to she should do it with the most exquisite grace; the fourth, that she should dance divinely; the fifth, that she should sing like a nightingale; and the sixth, that she should be complete mistress of every sort of musical instrument. Then came the evil fairy's turn. Shaking her head – more through spite than through age – she said that the princess would one day prick her finger with a spindle, and die forthwith.

This terrible prophecy made the whole company shudder, and there was no one present who did not feel ready to cry. Just in the nick of time, the young fairy came out from behind the tapestry. 'Reassure yourselves, king and queen!' said she, speaking at the top of her voice. 'Your daughter shall not die. It is true that I have not the power to prevent altogether what my old friend has decreed. The princess will, indeed, prick her finger with a spindle; but, instead of dying, she shall only fall into a profound sleep, which shall last a hundred years, at the end of which time a king's son shall come and wake her from it.'

The king, who did all he could to ward off the doom pronounced by the old fairy, issued an edict forbidding any one to use a spindle, or even to have one in the house, on pain of death.

After fifteen or sixteen years, while the king and queen had gone to one of their pleasure-houses, it so happened that the princess was playing in the castle, running through the rooms and climbing up stairway after stairway. At last she came to the very top of a turret, and found herself in a little garret, where an old woman sat all alone working with her spindle.

'What are you doing there, my good woman?' said the princess.'

'I am spinning, my pretty child,' answered the old lady, who did not appear to recognize her.

'Oh! how nice it looks,' exclaimed the princess; 'how do you manage it? Do give it me, and let me see if I can do it as well as you.'

No sooner had she taken the spindle, catching hold if it a little roughly in her eagerness – or perhaps it was only the decree of the fairies that ordained it so – than it pricked her finger, and she fell in a swoon to the ground.

The good old lady, who seemed in a great state of alarm, cried for help. From every side the servants came running. One of them threw water in the princess's face. Another loosened her collar. Another slapped her hands. Another bathed her forehead with scented Queen-of-Hungary water. But nothing would restore her.

Then the king, who had come back to the palace, and rushed upstairs as soon as he heard the noise, remembered the prophecy of the fairies. Judging shrewdly enough that this was bound to happen, since the fairies had said so, he had the princess put in the most beautiful room in the palace, upon a bed embroidered with gold and silver. You would have said it was an angel lying there, so lovely was she, for her swoon had not robbed her complexion of its glowing tints. Her cheeks were still rosy, and her lips like coral. Her eyes were shut, but you could hear her soft breathing, and see clearly enough that she was not dead.

He gave orders that the princess should be left to sleep undisturbed until the time for her awakening should come.

The good fairy who had saved her life by dooming her to sleep for a hundred years was in the kingdom of Mataquin, twelve thousand leagues away, when the accident happened to the princess; but the news was soon brought to her by a little dwarf, who had seven-league boots, so that he could go seven leagues at each step. The fairy started off at once, and before an hour was over she had arrived, in her chariot of fire drawn by dragons, and had come down in the courtyard of the castle. The king went to her, and gave her his hand to help her out of the chariot. She approved of everything he had done, but as she was very far-seeing, she thought that when the princess should come to awake she would be frightened at finding herself all alone in the old castle. What was to be done? How could this be avoided? The fairy soon found a way out of the difficulty.

She touched with her wand everyone who was in the castle

except the king and queen – governesses, ladies-in-waiting, chambermaids, courtiers, officers, stewards, cooks, scullions, errand-boys, guards, beadles, pages, footmen. She touched also all the horses that were in the stables – with the grooms – the big mastiffs in the stable-yard, and little 'Puff,' the princess's tiny lap-dog, who lay close to her on the bed. The very moment that she touched them they all went off to sleep also, not to wake until such time as their mistress should wake too, so that they could attend upon her when necessary. Even the spits which were turning at the fire, laden with partridges and pheasants – they went to sleep as well, and the very fire itself. The fairy did not take long over her work.

Then the king and queen, having kissed their much-loved daughter without waking her, left the castle, and published a proclamation that no one was to approach it, whoever they might be. The proclamation proved quite needless, for in a quarter of an hour there had grown all round the park such a vast number of trees, large and small, of brambles and of briars all intertwined one with the other, that neither man nor beast could have made a way through them. So thick and high was the growth that you could see nothing more than just the tips of the castle towers, and that only from a long way off. You may take it for granted that this was another piece of the fairy's handiwork, and all arranged so that the princess, while she slept, should have nothing to fear from inquisitive strangers.

At the end of a hundred years, the son of a king who was reigning at that time, and who did not belong to the same family as the sleeping princess, was hunting in the neighbourhood, and asked what those towers were that he saw peeping up above a dense forest. Each told him just what each had heard.

Some said it was an old castle haunted by spirits; others that all the sorcerers in the country gathered there to celebrate their rites. The most common belief was that an ogre lived there, who carried thither all the children he could lay hands on, and ate them at his leisure, without anyone being able to follow him, because he alone was able to force his way through the wood.

The prince was wondering what to think when a peasant came forward. 'Fifty years ago, my prince,' said the peasant, 'my father told me that there was a princess in the castle – the most beautiful princess ever seen – who was to sleep for a hundred years. He told me, too, that she would be wakened by a king's son, whose bride she was destined to be.'

When he heard this, the young prince was on fire with eagerness. Without worrying about any difficulties, he believed the adventure as good as accomplished, and, urged forward by thoughts of love and of glory, resolved to see straight away what was to be found there. Hardly had he reached the outskirts of the wood, when all the great trees, the brambles and the briars, parted of their own accord to let him pass through. He marched onwards to the castle, which he saw at the end of a great avenue, down which he duly made his way. It surprised him a little, however, to notice that none of his companions had been able to follow him, because the trees closed together again as soon as he had gone past. But a young man – and a prince and lover to boot – is ever valiant! He did not allow himself to pause in his path, and soon came to a large outer court. Here everything that he cast his eye upon was of a sort to make his blood run cold. Over all was a fearful silence. The semblance of death met his gaze on every side – nothing but the stretched-out bodies of men and animals, all of them to every appearance dead. It was not long, however, before he recognized by the bulbous noses and still red faces of the porters that they were only asleep. Their glasses, where some drops of wine still lingered, served to show that they must have gone to sleep in the very act of drinking.

He passed a large court paved with marble. He mounted the staircase; he entered the hall of the guards, who were drawn up in a row, their carbines on their shoulders, snoring for all they were worth. He went through several rooms full of lords and ladies, all asleep, some upright, others sitting down.

At last he entered a gilded room, where he saw upon a bed – the curtains of which were open at each side – the most beautiful sight that he had ever known, the figure of a young girl, who seemed to be about fifteen or sixteen years old. Her beauty seemed to shine with an almost unearthly radiance. He drew near in trembling wonder, and knelt down by her side.

Just then, as the end of her enchantment was come, the princess awoke, and looking at him with a glance more tender than a moment's acquaintance would seem to warrant, said 'Is it you, my prince? How long you have kept me waiting!'

The prince, charmed with these words, and still more with the manner in which they were spoken, did not know how to express his joy. He assured her that he loved her more than himself. They did not use any fine phrases, these two, but they were none the less happy on that account. Where love is, what need of eloquence? He was more at a loss than she, and small

The Sleeping Beauty *opposite*: Then came the evil fairy's turn. She said that the princess would one day prick her finger with a spindle and die forthwith.

The Good and Bad
Fairies at the
Christening of the
Princess Beauty

The Prince awakens
the SLEEPING BEAUTY

wonder? She had had plenty of time to think over what she was going to say! Anyhow, they talked together for four hours, and they had not even then said half of what was in their hearts.

'Can it be, beautiful princess,' said the prince, looking at her with eyes that told a thousand things more than tongue could utter, 'can it be that some kindly fate ordained that I should be born expressly for you? Can it be that these beautiful eyes only open for me – that all the kings of the earth, with all their power, could not do what my love has done?'

'Yes, my dear prince,' replied the princess; 'I knew at first sight that we were born for each other. It is you that I saw, that I talked with, that I loved, all through my long sleep. It was with your image that the fairy filled my dreams. I knew that he who would come to free me from my spell would be lovelier than love itself; that he would love me more than his own life; and when you came to me, I recognised him in you.'

In the meantime, everybody in the palace had woken up at the same moment as the princess. Each began worrying about his or her duties, and as they were not all lovers, they began to remember that it was a long time since they had had anything to eat, and that they were ready to die with hunger. The lady-in-waiting, as famished as the rest, grew impatient, and called to the princess that supper was ready.

The prince helped the princess to get up. She was fully and very magnificently dressed; but he was careful not to remind her that her ruff and farthingale were after the fashion of his

The Sleeping Beauty *opposite*: At last he entered a gilded room, where he saw upon a bed the most beautiful sight that he has ever known – the figure of a young girl, whose beauty seemed to shine with an almost unearthly radiance.

grandmother's time. She was none the less beautiful for that.

They passed into a saloon with mirrors all round the walls, and there they had supper. The musicians, with fiddles and oboes, played some old pieces of music, excellent in their way, though a hundred years had gone by since they were heard last. After supper, without losing any time, the chief chaplain married the prince and princess in the chapel, and they retired to rest. They slept little. The princess, to be sure, after her hundred years, had no great need of sleep, and as soon as morning broke the prince left her, and returned to the town, for he knew the king, his father, would be growing anxious about him.

The prince told him that, when hunting, he had been lost in the forest, had spent the night in a charcoal-burners' hut, and had made his supper of black bread and cheese. The king, his father, who was an easy-going fellow, believed him; but the queen, his mother, would not be so easily persuaded. She noticed that the prince was always going hunting, and seemed always to have some excuse or other for staying away several days; and she had a shrewd suspicion that he had a sweetheart somewhere or other. She often tried to get him to tell her about it by hinting that he should be contented with life at the palace; but he never dared trust her with his secret. He feared her, although he loved her. For she came of a family of ogresses, and the king had only married her for her wealth. It used even to be whispered at the court that she herself had all the instincts of an ogress, and that when she saw any little children passing by she had to hold herself back to keep from rushing at them. So the prince thought it best not to tell her anything at all. For two years he continued seeing his beloved princess in secret, and he loved her always more and more. The air of mystery about it all made him fall in love with her afresh each time he saw her, and homely joys did not lessen the warmth of his passion.

So when the king, his father, was dead, and he saw himself master, he declared his marriage publicly, and went in full state to visit the queen, his wife, in her castle. It was with all possible pomp and ceremony that he now made his entry into what was, after all, the old capital of the country.

Some time after he had become king, the prince went to make war upon his neighbour, the Emperor Cantalabutte. He left the management of the kingdom in the hands of the queen, his mother, and told her to be kind to the young queen, whom he loved all the more since she had brought him two pretty children – a girl and a boy – whom he called Dawn and Day, because they were so beautiful. The king was to be away at the war all the summer, and no sooner had he gone than the queen-mother sent her daughter-in-law and the children to a country house in the woods, where she could more easily satisfy her horrible craving.

She went there herself some days afterwards, and said one evening to her steward: 'Master Simon, to-morrow I mean to eat little Dawn for my dinner.'

'Oh, madam!' said the steward.

'I wish it,' replied the queen-mother, in the tones of an ogress, hungry for fresh young victims.

The poor man, seeing that it would be no use trying to thwart an ogress, took his big knife and went up to little Dawn's room. She was just four years old, and she ran to him, laughing and skipping, and threw her arms round his neck, and asked him if he had brought her some candies. The knife fell from his hands, and he went to the yard, and cut the throat of a little lamb instead. This he served up with some sauce, which was so delightful that the queen-mother vowed she had never tasted anything better in her life. In the meantime, he carried off little Dawn, and gave her to his wife, who hid her in their own quarters at the bottom of the yard.

About a week afterwards, the wicked queen-mother said to her steward: 'Master Simon, I want to eat little Day for my supper.'

He did not reply at all, but, resolving to deceive her again, went to look for little Day, and found him with a tiny sword in his hand, with which he was pretending to fence a huge ape. He was only three years old. The steward carried the boy to his wife, who hid him with little Dawn; and he served up instead to the wicked queen-mother a tender little goat, which she found admirable fare.

So all was well, so far as that was concerned; but one evening the wicked old queen called out in a terrible voice: 'Master Simon! Master Simon!' He went to her immediately. 'To-morrow,' said she, 'I want to eat my daughter-in-law.'

Then at last Master Simon despaired of being still able to hoodwink the old ogress. The young queen was now some twenty years old, without counting the hundred years that she had slept. How should he get an animal to replace her? He decided that there was nothing for it. To save his own life, he must cut the young queen's throat, and he went up to her room determined to finish the business there and then. Working himself up into a suitable frenzy, he entered the young queen's room. He did not wish, however, to take her altogether by surprise; so with great respect he told her of the orders he had received from the queen-mother.

'Kill me! kill me!' said she, offering him her neck; 'fulfil the command that has been given you. I shall only be going to see my children again – my poor children, whom I loved so well!' She believed them dead.

'No, no, madam!' replied poor Master Simon, his heart softening, 'you shall not die. You shall go to see your dear children again; but it shall be in my house, where I am keeping them in hiding. I will trick the old queen once more. I will make her eat a young deer in your place.'

He took her without more ado to his wife's room, where he left her clasping her children in her arms and crying with them, and went to prepare the deer, which the ogress ate for her supper with just as much gusto as if it had indeed been the young queen. She was, in fact, quite delighted over her own cruelty, and had made up her mind to tell the king that some ravenous wolves had eaten his wife and his two children.

One evening, while the old queen was roaming about the courts and yards of the castle to see if she could sniff out some fresh dainty, she heard in one of the back rooms little Day, who was crying because his mother was going to whip him for being naughty. She also heard little Dawn asking forgiveness for her brother. The ogress recognized the voices of the young queen and her children. Furious at having been duped, she commanded – in that terrible voice of hers that frightened everybody – that on the very next morning a huge tub should be brought into the middle of the courtyard. It should be filled with toads, vipers, adders, and all sorts of reptiles, and the young queen and children, Master Simon, his wife, and servant were all to be thrown in together. They were to be brought thither – so the old queen commanded – with their hands tied.

They were already there – the executioners stood in readiness to throw them into the tub – when the young queen asked that at least she should be allowed to bid her children farewell, and the ogress, wicked as she was, consented. 'Alas, alas!' cried the poor princess, 'must I die so young? It is true that I have been a good while in the world, but I have slept a hundred years, and surely that ought not to count! What will you say, what will you do, my poor prince, when you come back, and find that your little Day, who is so sweet, and your little Dawn, who is so pretty, are there no longer to throw their little arms round your neck, and that even I myself am no longer there to greet you? If I weep, it is your tears that I shed. Perhaps – I dread to think it – you will take vengeance for our fate upon yourself! As for you, miserable wretches, who do an ogress's bidding, the king will have you put to death.'

The ogress, when she heard these words – which went so far beyond a mere farewell – was transported with rage, and cried: 'Executioners, do your duty, and throw this babbler into the tub!' They there and then took hold the young queen.

But, just at that moment, the king, whom no one expected to arrive so early, came riding into the courtyard. He had come posthaste; he asked, in his astonishment, what was the meaning of this horrible sight. No one dared to tell him. The ogress, maddened at seeing the course events had taken, threw herself head foremost into the tub, and was gobbled up in an instant.

The king did not allow himself to be grieved overmuch, although she was his mother. He soon found consolation in his beautiful wife and his children.

Henny-Penny

ne day Henny-penny was picking up corn in the cornyard when – whack! – something hit her upon the head. 'Goodness gracious me!' said Henny-penny; 'the sky's a-going to fall; I must go and tell the king.'

So she went along and she went along and she went along till she met Cocky-locky.

'Where are you going, Henny-penny?' said Cocky-locky.

'Oh! I'm going to tell the king the sky's a-falling,' said Henny-penny.

'May I come with you?' said Cocky-locky.

'Certainly,' said Henny-penny. So Henny-penny and Cocky-locky went to tell the king the sky was a-falling.

They went along, and they went along, and they went along, till they met Ducky-daddles.

'Where are you going to, Henny-penny and Cocky-locky?' said Ducky-daddles.

'Oh! we're going to tell the king the sky's a-falling,' said Henny-penny and Cocky-locky.

'May I come with you?' said Ducky-daddles.

'Certainly,' said Henny-penny and Cocky-locky. So Henny-penny, Cocky-locky and Ducky-daddles went to tell the king the sky was a-falling.

So they went along, and they went along, and they went along, till they met Goosey-poosey.

'Where are you going to, Henny-penny, Cocky-locky and Ducky-daddles?' said Goosey-poosey.

'Oh! we're going to tell the king the sky's a-falling,' said Henny-Penny and Cocky-locky and Ducky-daddles.

'May I come with you?' said Goosey-poosey.

'Certainly,' said Henny-penny, Cocky-locky and Ducky-daddles. So Henny-penny, Cocky-locky, Ducky-daddles and Goosey-poosey went to tell the king the sky was a-falling.

So they went along, and they went along, and they went along, till they met Turkey-lurkey.

'Where are you going, Henny-penny, Cocky-locky, Ducky-daddles, and Goosey-poosey?' said Turkey-lurkey.

'Oh! we're going to tell the king the sky's a-falling,' said Henny-penny, Cocky-locky, Ducky-daddles and Goosey-poosey.

'May I come with you, Henny-penny, Cocky-locky, Ducky-daddles and Goosey-poosey?' said Turkey-lurkey.

'Why, certainly, Turkey-lurkey,' said Henny-penny, Cocky-locky, Ducky-daddles, and Goosey-poosey. So Henny-penny, Cocky-locky, Ducky-daddles, Goosey-poosey and Turkey-lurkey all went to tell the king the sky was a-falling.

So they went along, and they went along, and they went along, till they met Foxy-woxy, and Foxy-woxy said to Henny-penny, Cocky-locky, Ducky-daddles, Goosey-poosey and Turkey-lurkey: 'Where are you going, Henny-penny, Cocky-locky, Ducky-daddles, Goosey-poosey and Turkey-lurkey?'

And Henny-penny, Cocky-locky, Ducky-daddles, Goosey-poosey, and Turkey-lurkey said to Foxy-woxy: 'We're going to tell the king the sky's a falling.'

'Oh! but this is not the way to the king, Henny-penny, Cocky-locky, Ducky-daddles, Goosey-poosey and Turkey-lurkey,' said Foxy-woxy; 'I know the proper way; shall I show it to you?''

'Why certainly, Foxy-woxy,' said Henny-penny, Cocky-locky, Ducky-daddles, Goosey-poosey, and Turkey-lurkey. So Henny-penny, Cocky-locky, Ducky-daddles, Goosey-poosey, Turkey-lurkey, and Foxy-woxy all went to tell the king the sky was a-falling.

So they went along, and they went along, and they went along, till they came to a narrow and dark hole. Now this was the door of Foxy-woxy's cave. But Foxy-woxy said to Henny-penny, Cocky-locky, Ducky-daddles, Goosey-poosey, and Turkey-lurkey: 'This is the short way to the king's palace; you'll soon get there if you follow me. I will go first and you come after, Henny-penny, Cocky-locky, Ducky-daddles, Goosey-poosey, and Turkey-lurkey.'

'Why of course, certainly, without doubt, why not?' said Henny-penny, Cocky-locky, Ducky-daddles, Goosey-poosey, and Turkey-lurkey.

So Foxy-woxy went into his cave, and he didn't go very far, but turned round to wait for Henny-penny, Cocky-locky, Ducky-daddles, Goosey-poosey and Turkey-lurkey. So at last Turkey-lurkey first went through the dark hole into the cave. He hadn't got far when 'Hrumph,' Foxy-woxy snapped off Turkey-lurkey's head and threw his body over his left shoulder. Then Goosey-poosey went in, and 'Hrumph,' off went her head and Goosey-poosey was thrown beside Turkey-lurkey. Then Ducky-daddles waddled down, and 'Hrumph,' snapped Foxy-woxy, and Ducky-daddles' head was off and Ducky-daddles was thrown alongside Turkey-lurkey and Goosey-poosey. Then Cocky-locky strutted down into the cave and he hadn't gone far when 'Snap, Hrumph!' went Foxy-woxy and Cocky-locky was thrown alongside of Turkey-lurkey, Goosey-poosey and Ducky-daddles.

But Foxy-woxy had made two bites at Cocky-locky, and when the first snap only hurt Cocky-locky, but didn't kill him, he called out to Henny-penny. So she turned tail and ran back home, and she never told the king the sky was a-falling.

Hansel and Gretel

nce upon a time there dwelt near a large wood a poor woodcutter, with his wife and two children by his former marriage, a little boy called Hansel and a girl named Gretel. He had little enough to break or bite; and once, when there was a great famine in the land, he could not procure even his daily bread; and as he lay thinking in his bed one evening, rolling about with worry, he sighed, and said to his wife, 'What will become of us? How can we feed our children, when we have no more than we can eat ourselves?'

'Know, then, my husband,' answered she, 'we will lead them away quite early in the morning into the thickest part of the wood, and there make them a fire, and give them each a little piece of bread; then we will go to our work, and leave them alone, so they will not find the way home again, and we shall be freed from them.'

'No, wife,' replied he, 'that I can never do. How can you bring your heart to leave my children all alone in the wood, for the wild beasts will soon come and tear them to pieces?'

'Oh, you simpleton!' said she. 'Then we must all four die of hunger; you had better make the coffins for us.'

But she left him no peace till he consented, saying, 'Ah, but I shall regret the poor children.'

The two children, however, had not gone to sleep because they were so hungry, and so they overheard what the stepmother said to their father. Gretel wept bitterly, and cried out to Hansel, 'What ever will become of us, Hansel?'

'Be quiet, Gretel,' said he. 'Do not cry – I will soon help you.'

And as soon as their parents had fallen asleep he got up, put on his coat, and, unbarring the back-door, slipped out. The moon shone brightly, and the white pebbles which lay before the door seemed like silver coins, they glittered so brightly. Hansel stooped down, and put as many into his pocket as it would hold; and then going back he said to Gretel, 'Be comforted, dear sister, and sleep in peace; God will not forsake us.' So saying he went to bed again.

The next morning before the sun arose the wife went and awoke the children. 'Get up, you lazy things; we are going into the forest to chop wood.' Then she gave them each a piece of bread, saying, 'There is something for your dinner. Do not eat it before the time, for you will get nothing else.'

Gretel took the bread in her apron, for Hansel's pocket was full of pebbles; and so they all set out upon their way. When they had gone a little distance Hansel stood still, and peeped back at the house; and this he repeated several times, till his father said, 'Hansel, what are you peeping at, and why do you lag behind? Take care, and remember your legs.'

'Ah, Father,' said Hansel, 'I am looking at my white cat sitting upon the roof of the house, trying to say good-bye.'

'You simpleton!' said the wife. 'That is not a cat; it is only the sun shining on the white chimney. In reality Hansel was not looking at a cat; but every time he stopped he dropped a pebble out of his pocket upon the path.

When they came to the middle of the wood the father told the children to collect wood, and he would make them a fire, so that they should not be cold. So Hansel and Gretel gathered together quite a little mountain of twigs. Then they set fire to them; and as the flame burnt up high the wife said, 'Now, you children, lie down near the fire and rest yourselves, while we go into the forest and chop wood. 'When we are ready I will come and call you.'

Hansel and Gretel sat down by the fire, and when it was noon each ate the piece of bread; and because they could hear the blows of an axe they thought their father was near; it was not an axe, but a branch which he had bound to a withered tree, so as to be blown to and fro by the wind. They waited so long that at last their eyes closed from weariness, and they fell fast asleep. When they awoke it was quite dark, and Gretel began to cry, 'How shall we get out of the wood?'

Hansel tried to comfort her by saying, 'Wait a little while till the moon rises, and then we will quickly find the way.'

The moon soon shone forth, and Hansel, taking his sister's hand, followed the pebbles, which glittered like new silver coins and showed them the path. All night long they walked on, and as day broke they came to their father's house.

They knocked at the door, and when the wife opened it and saw Hansel and Gretel she exclaimed, 'You wicked children! Why did you sleep so long in the wood? We thought you were never coming home again.' But their father was very glad, for it had grieved his heart to leave them all alone.

Not long afterwards there was again great scarcity in every corner of the land; and one night the children overheard their step-mother saying to their father, 'Everything is again consumed; we have only half a loaf left, and then the song is ended; the children must be sent away. We will take them deeper into the wood, so that they may not find the way out again. It is the only means of escape for us.'

But her husband felt heavy at heart, and thought, 'It is better to share the last crust with the children.' His wife, however, would listen to nothing that he said, and scolded and reproached him without end.

He who says *A*, must say *B* too; and he who consents the first time, must also the second.

The children, however, had heard the conversation as they lay awake, and as soon as the old people went to sleep Hansel got up, intending to pick up some pebbles as before; but the wife had locked the door, so that he could not get out. Nevertheless he comforted Gretel, saying, 'Do not cry; sleep in quiet; the good God will not forsake us.'

Early in the morning the step-mother came and pulled them out of bed, and gave them each a slice of bread, which was even smaller than the former piece. On the way Hansel broke his in his pocket, and, stooping every now and then, dropped a crumb upon the path.

'Hansel, why do you stop and look about?' said the father. 'Keep in the path.'

'I am looking at my little dove,' answered Hansel, 'nodding a good-bye to me.'

'Simpleton!' said the wife. 'That is no dove, but only the sun shining on the chimney.' But Hansel still kept dropping crumbs as he went along.

The step-mother led the children deep into the wood, where they had never been before, and there making an immense fire she said to them, 'Sit down here and rest, and when you feel tired you can sleep for a little while. We are going into the forest to hew wood, and in the evening, when we are ready, we will come and get you and we will all go home together.'

When noon came Gretel shared her bread with Hansel, who had strewn his on the path. Then they went to sleep; but the evening arrived, and no one came to visit the poor children; in the dark night they awoke, and Hansel comforted his sister by saying, 'Only wait, Gretel, till the moon comes out; then we shall see the crumbs of bread which I have dropped, and they will show us the way home.'

The moon shone and they got up, but they could not see any crumbs, for the thousands of birds which had been flying about in the woods and fields had picked them all up. Hansel kept saying to Gretel, 'We will soon find the way'; but they did not, and they walked the whole night long and the next day, but still they did not come out of the wood; and they got so hungry, for they had nothing to eat but the berries which they found upon the bushes. Soon they got so tired that they could not drag themselves along, so they lay down under a tree and went to sleep.

It was now the third morning since they had left their father's house, and they still walked on; but they only got deeper and deeper into the wood, and Hansel saw that if help did not come very soon they would die of hunger. As soon as it was noon they saw a beautiful snow-white bird sitting upon a bough, which sang so sweetly that they stood still and listened to it. It soon left off, and spreading its wings flew off; and they followed it until it arrived at a cottage, upon the roof of which it perched; and when they went close up to it they saw that the cottage was made of bread and cakes, and the window-panes were of clear sugar.

'We will go in there,' said Hansel, 'and have a glorious feast.

I will eat a piece of the roof, and you can eat the window. Will they not be sweet?'

So Hansel reached up and broke a piece off the roof, in order to see how it tasted; while Gretel stepped up to the window and began to bite it.

Then a sweet voice called out in the room, 'Tip-tap, tip-tap, who raps at my door?'

The children answered, 'The wind, the wind, the child of heaven'; and they went on eating the sugar and cake and bread without interruption.

Hansel thought the roof tasted very nice, and so he tore off a great piece, while Gretel broke a large round pane out of the window, and sat down quite comfortably and contentedly to eat every last bit of it.

Just then the door opened, and a very old woman walking upon crutches came out. Hansel and Gretel were so frightened that they let fall what they had in their hands; but the old woman, nodding her head, said, 'Ah, you dear children, what has brought you here? Come in and stop with me, and no harm shall befall you.' So saying she took them both by the hand, and let them into her cottage. A good meal of milk and pancakes, with sugar, apples, and nuts, was spread on the table, and in the back-room were two nice little beds, covered with white blankets, where Hansel and Gretel laid themselves down and thought themselves in heaven.

The old woman behaved very kindly to them, but in reality she was a wicked witch who waylaid children, and had built the bread-house in order to entice them in; but as soon as they were in her power she killed them, cooked and ate them, and made a great festival of the day. Did you know that witches have red eyes, and cannot see very far; but they have a fine sense of smell, like wild beasts, so that they know when children approach them?

When she first saw Hansel and Gretel come near the witch's house she laughed wickedly, saying, 'Here come two who shall not escape me.' And early in the morning before they awoke she went up to them, and saw how lovingly they lay sleeping, with their chubby red cheeks; and she mumbled to herself, 'That will be a good bite.' Then she took up Hansel with her rough hand, and shut him up in a little cage with a lattice-door; and although he screamed loudly, it was of no use. Gretel came next, and, shaking her till she awoke, she said, 'Get up, you lazy thing, and fetch some water to cook something good for your brother, who must remain in that stall and get fat. When he is fat enough I shall eat him.' Gretel began to cry, but it was all useless, for the old witch made her do as she wished. So a nice meal was cooked for Hansel, but Gretel got nothing else but a crab's claw.

Every morning the old witch came to the cage and said, 'Hansel, stretch out your finger, that I may feel whether you are getting fat.' But Hansel used to stretch out a bone, and the old woman, having very bad sight, thought it was his finger, and wondered very much that he did not get fatter.

When four weeks had passed and Hansel still kept quite lean she lost all her patience, and would not wait any longer. 'Gretel,' the wicked witch called out in a raging passion, 'get some water quickly! Be Hansel fat or lean, this morning I will kill and cook him.'

Oh, how the poor little sister grieved as she was forced to fetch the water, and fast the tears ran down her cheeks! 'Dear, good God, help us now!' she exclaimed. 'Had we only been eaten by the wild beasts in the wood, then we should have died together.'

But the old witch called out, 'Leave off that noise: it will not help you a bit.'

So early in the morning Gretel was forced to go out and fill the kettle and make a fire. 'First we will bake, however,' said the old woman. 'I have already heated the oven and kneaded the dough.' So saying, she pushed poor Gretel up to the oven, out of which the flames were burning fiercely. 'Creep in,' said the witch, 'and see if it is hot enough, and then we will put in the bread.' But she intended when Gretel got in to shut up the oven and let her bake, so that she might eat her as well as Hansel.

Gretel perceived what her thoughts were, and said, 'I do not know how to do it. How shall I get in?'

'You stupid goose!' said she. 'The opening is big enough. See, I could even get in myself!' And she got up, and put her head into the oven.

Then Gretel gave her a push, so that she fell right in, and then shutting the iron door she bolted it. Oh, how horribly she howled! But Gretel ran away, and left the ungodly witch to burn to ashes.

Now she ran to Hansel, and, opening his door, called out, 'Hansel, we are saved; the old witch is dead!' So he sprang out, like a bird out of his cage when the door is opened; and they were so glad that they fell upon each other's neck, and kissed each other over and over again. They laughed and they cried and they hugged each other as tightly as can be.

And now, as there was nothing to fear, they went into the

witch's house, where in every corner were caskets full of pearls and precious stones. 'These are better than pebbles,' said Hansel, putting as many into his pocket as it would hold; while Gretel thought, 'I will take some home too,' and filled her apron full of pearls and precious stones.

'We must be off now,' said Hansel, 'and get out of this enchanted forest'; but when they had walked for two hours they came to a large piece of water. 'We cannot get over,' said Hansel. 'I can see no bridge at all.'

'And there is no boat either,' said Gretel, 'but there swims a white duck. I will ask her to help us over.' Then Gretel sang so sweetly:

'Little Duck, good little Duck,
Gretel and Hansel, here we stand,
There is neither stile nor bridge;
Take us on your back to land.'

So the Duck came to them, and Hansel sat himself on, and bade his sister sit behind him.

'No,' answered Gretel, 'that will be too much for the Duck; she shall take us over one at a time. You go first and I will wait here. I know the good little Duck will come back for me.'

This the good little bird did, and when both were happily arrived on the other side and had gone a little way they came to a well-known wood, which they knew the better every step they went, and at last they saw their father's house. Then they began to run, and, bursting into the house, they fell on their father's neck. He had not had one happy hour since he had left the children in the forest; and his wife was dead. Gretel shook her apron, and the pearls and precious stones rolled out upon the floor, and Hansel threw down one handful after the other out of his pocket. Then all their sorrows were ended, and Hansel and Gretel lived together in great happiness with their dear father who they loved so much.

My tale is done. There runs a mouse: whoever catches her may make a great, great cap out of her fur.

Hansel and Gretel *opposite*: They saw that the cottage was made of bread and cakes, and the window-panes were of clear sugar. 'We will go in there,' said Hansel, 'and have a glorious feast. I will eat a piece of the roof, and you can eat the window. Will they not be sweet?'

"Pull the bobbin, and the latch will go up."

Little Red Riding-Hood

nce upon a time there was a little village-girl, the prettiest ever seen; her mother doted upon her, and so did her grandmother. She, good woman, made for her a little red hood which suited her so well, that everyone called her Little Red Riding-Hood.

One day her mother, who had just made some cakes, said to her: 'My dear, you shall go and see how your grandmother is, for I have heard she is ailing; take her this cake and this little pot of butter. Go quickly, and don't talk to strangers on the way.'

Little Red Riding Hood started off at once for her grandmother's cottage, which was in another village.

While passing through a wood she walked slowly, often stopping to pick flowers. She looked back and saw a wolf approaching, so she stopped and waited. The wolf, who would very much liked to have eaten her, dared not, because some woodcutters were near by in the forest. So he said 'Good morning, Red Riding-Hood. Where are you going?'

Little Red Riding-Hood *page 66*: She looked back and saw a wolf approaching, so she stopped and waited.

Little Red-Riding Hood *page 67*: The wolf would very much like to have eaten her, but dared not, because some woodcutters were near by in the forest.

Little Red-Riding Hood *opposite*: 'Who's there?' called out the wolf in a gruff voice. ''Tis your grand-daughter, Little Red Riding-Hood, and I have brought you a cake and a little pot of butter that my mother sends you.' 'Pull the bobbin, and the latch will go up.'

The poor child, who did not know it was dangerous to talk to a wolf, answered, 'I am going to see my grandmother, to take her a cake and a little pot of butter that my mother sends her.'

'Does she live a great way off?' said the wolf.

'Oh, yes!' said Little Red Riding-Hood, 'she lives beyond the mill you see right down there in the first house in the village.'

'Well,' said the wolf, 'I shall go and see her too. I shall take this road, and you take that one, and let us see who will get there first!'

The wolf set off at a gallop along the shortest road; but the little girl took the longest way and amused herself by gathering nuts, running after butterflies, and plucking daisies and buttercups.

The wolf soon reached her grandmother's cottage; he knocked at the door – *rap, rap.*

'Who's there?'

' 'Tis your grand-daughter, Little Red Riding-Hood,' said the wolf in a shrill voice, 'and I have brought you a cake and a little pot of butter that my mother sends you.'

The good old grandmother, who was ill in bed, called out, 'Pull the bobbin, and the latch will go up!'

The wolf pulled the bobbin and the door opened. He leaped on the old woman and gobbled her up in a minute; for he had had no dinner for three days past.

Then he shut the door and rolled himself up in the grand-mother's bed, to wait for Little Red Riding-Hood.

In a while she came knocking at the door – *rap, rap.*

'Who's there?'

Little Red Riding-Hood, who heard the gruff voice of the wolf, was frightened at first, but thinking that her grandmother had a cold, answered, ' 'Tis your grand-daughter, Little Red Riding-Hood, and I have brought you a cake and a little pot of butter that my mother sends you.'

Then the wolf called to her in as soft a voice as he could, 'Pull the bobbin, and the latch will go up.' Little Red Riding-Hood pulled the bobbin and the door opened.

When the wolf saw her come in he covered himself up with the sheets, and said, 'Put the cake and the little pot of butter on the chest, and come and lie down beside me.'

Little Red Riding-Hood went over to the bed; she was surprised to see how strange her grandmother looked in her nightcap. But she took off her cloak and hung it up, then went back and sat down by the bed. She looked at her grandmother again with great interest.

She said to her, 'Oh, grandmamma, grandmamma, what great arms you have got!'

'All the better to hug you with, my dear!'

'Oh, grandmamma, grandmamma, what great legs you have got!' she said.

'All the better to run with, my dear!'

'Oh grandmamma, grandmamma, what great ears you have got!' said the little girl.

'All the better to hear you with, my dear!'

'Oh grandmamma, grandmamma, what great eyes you have got!' she said, beginning to get frightened.

'All the better to see you with, my dear!'

'Oh, grandmamma, grandmamma, what great *teeth* you have got!' said Little Red Riding-Hood.

'All the better to gobble you up!' said the wicked wolf,

suddenly sitting up in the bed, drooling with hunger.

Little Red Riding Hood screamed with terror and leapt up from her chair. Then a shot from a gun was heard, and the wicked wolf dropped back in the bed dead.

A woodcutter who was passing had heard the cries of Little Red Riding-Hood, popped his gun through the window and shot the wolf in time to save her. The woodcutter rushed into the cottage and picked up Little Red Riding-Hood, who was trembling with fright. She was able to tell the woodcutter, between her tears, that the wolf had eaten up her grandmother. Quick as a wink, the woodcutter cut open the wolf's stomach and rescued the old lady, who soon recovered from her dreadful experience. She thanked the woodcutter for his timely arrival, and for saving both her and Little Red Riding-Hood. They both waved goodbye, when he left to go back to his work in the forest.

The old lady hugged her dear little grand-daughter and asked if she might have a cup of tea, please.

'Yes, of course,' said Little Red Riding-Hood. She put the kettle on and put out the cake her mother had made on a pretty little plate. While she was waiting for the kettle to boil, she made her grandmother comfortable once more.

All Little Red Riding-Hood really wanted to do was to go home to her mother, for she was still very frightened by all that had happened. So she kissed her grandmother goodbye and ran all the way home. When she came to the cottage she found her mother waiting for her at the door.

Little Red Riding-Hood *opposite*: 'Oh, grandmamma, grandmamma, what great eyes you have got!' 'All the better to see you with, my dear.'

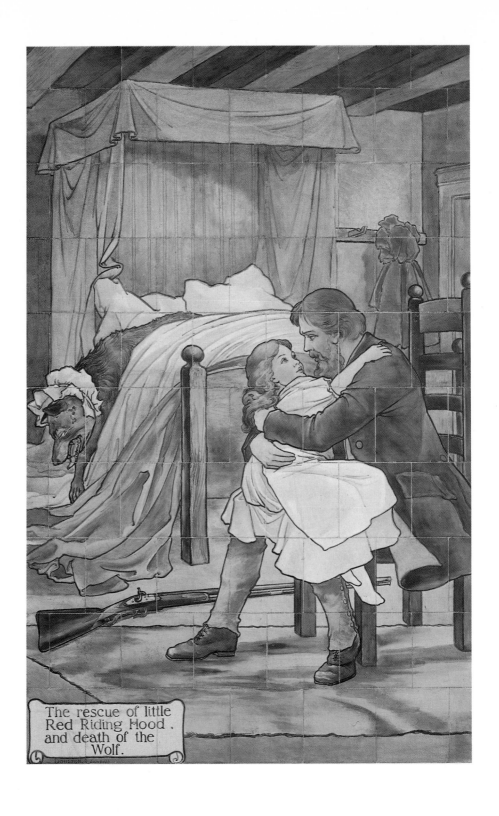

The rescue of little
Red Riding Hood,
and death of the
Wolf.

The mother drew Little Red Riding-Hood in, and listened to her story of all that had happened. She was delighted to have her little girl home safely again, and Little Red Riding-Hood was so happy to be out of danger that she promised her mother never to be disobedient any more.

Little Red Riding-Hood *opposite*: Suddenly, a shot from a gun was heard and the wicked wolf dropped back in the bed – dead. The woodcutter picked up Red Riding-Hood who was trembling with fright.

The Princess and the Pea

nce upon a time there was a prince, and, as he knew very well that he was a *real* prince and could never forget it for a single moment, he very naturally wanted to marry a *real* princess. He sought one after another, and, after talking about the weather and the health of the emperor, he found in each case that there was something about them he didn't like – something artificial and unprincess-like. When he spoke gently they smiled; when he spoke roughly to hurt them, they still smiled – the same smile. They were not a success. None of them was what he wanted. His princess must be so sensitive that she would wither at a reproachful glance; so delicately dainty that a spot of dust would make her scream; and, the draught of a fly's wings cause her a severe cold. He would have the real thing, or nothing.

When this exacting prince had duly considered all the princesses in his own country, and found them wanting, he set out to travel all over the world, forever saying to himself, 'I am a real prince: there *must* be a real princess somewhere.'

He found plenty of princesses on his travels, but when he spoke to them about the weather he soon found that they were not what he called *real* princesses. They were the daughters of kings and queens, yes, but –

Sad and weary he returned home with an empty heart. He had not found what he had set out to seek, yet he was firmly convinced that the world did contain such a thing as a real princess. He wanted her so badly, and that was how he knew that she must be there – somewhere.

And he was right.

One evening as he was sitting in his father's palace, studying books of far-off lands where princesses might be found, there came a fearful thunderstorm. The lightning grasped at the earth, spreading its roots down the walls of heaven; the thunder split and roared and rattled as if the ceiling was coming down; and, when the cloud-man unsealed his can and tipped it up, *swish* came the rain in torrents. Indeed, it was a fearful night.

When the storm had risen to the height of its fury a messenger came running to the king crying, 'Your Majesty gave orders that all gates be locked and barred, and opened to none; but someone without knocks and knocks and knocks, and will not go away.'

'I will go myself,' said the king, 'and see who it is that craves admittance in this fearful storm.'

So the king went down and opened the palace gates. He was astonished to see standing there a lovely maiden all forlorn, her long hair drenched with the rain, her beautiful clothes saturated and clinging to her form, while the water, trickling from them, ran out at her heels. She was in a terrible plight, but she was beautiful, and she said she was a princess – a real princess. Her mind was distracted: she could not remember how or whence she came, but, being a princess, and seeing the palace gates, she had run through the storm and knocked hard.

'A real princess,' said the king, looking her up and down 'Hm! I believe you, though the queen mightn't. Come in!'

The old queen received the visitor coldly and with a critical eye. 'We shall soon see if she is what she says she is,' thought the queen, but she said nothing. Then she went into the spare bedroom, and took off all the sheets and blankets, and laid a pea on the bedstead. On top of this she piled mattress after mattress to the number of twenty, and then twenty feather beds on top of that. 'Now,' she said to herself, 'here she shall sleep, and we shall soon see in the morning whether she is a real princess or not.'

So they put the princess to bed on the top of the twenty feather beds and as many mattresses, and said good-night.

In the morning they asked her how she had slept.

'Not at all,' replied she wearily; 'not a wink the whole night long. Heaven knows what there was in the bed. Whichever way I turned I still seemed to be lying upon some hard thing, and, I assure you, this morning my whole body's black and blue. It's terrible!'

Then the old queen told what she had done, and they all saw plainly that this was indeed a real princess when she could feel the pea through twenty feather beds and twenty mattresses. None but a real princess could possibly have such a delicate skin.

So the prince married her, quite satisfied that he had now found his real princess.

Now this is a true story, and if you don't believe it you have only to go and look at the pea itself, which is still carefully preserved in the museum – unless someone has stolen it.

The Golden Goose

here was a man who had three sons. The youngest was called Dummling, and was on all occasions despised and ill-treated by the whole family. It happened that the eldest took it into his head one day to go into the wood to cut trees for fuel; and his mother gave him a delicious meat pie and a bottle of wine to take with him, that he might refresh himself at his work.

As he went into the wood, a little old man bid him good day, and said, 'Give me a little piece of meat from your plate, and a little wine out of your bottle; I am very hungry and thirsty.'

But this clever young man said, 'Give you my meat and wine! No, I thank you; I should not have enough left for myself,' and away he went. He soon began to cut down a tree; but he had not worked long before he missed his stroke, and cut himself, and was obliged to go home to have the wound dressed. Now, it was the little old man that caused him this mischief.

Next the second son went out to work; and his mother gave him too a meat pie and a bottle of wine. And the same little old man met him also, and asked him for something to eat and drink.

But he too thought himself vastly clever, and said, 'Whatever you get, I shall lose; so go on your way!' The little man took care that he should have his reward; and the second stroke that he aimed against a tree, hit him on the leg; so that he too was forced to go home.

Then Dummling said, 'Father, I should like to go and cut wood too.'

But his father answered, 'Your brothers have both lamed themselves; you had better stay at home, for you know nothing of the business.' But Dummling was very pressing; and at last his father said, 'Go your way; you will be wiser when you have suffered for your folly.' And his mother gave him only some dry bread, and a bottle of sour beer; when he went into the wood, he met the little old man, who said, 'Give me some meat and drink, for I am very hungry and thirsty.'

Dummling said, 'I have only dry bread and sour beer; if that will suit you, we will sit down and eat it together.' So they sat down; and when the lad pulled out his bread, behold it was turned into an excellent meat pie, and his sour beer became delightful wine. They ate and drank heartily. When they had done, the little man said, 'As you have a kind heart, and have been willing to share everything with me, I will send a blessing upon you. There stands an old tree; cut it down, and you will find something at the root.' Then he went on his way.

Dummling set to work, and cut down the tree; and when it fell, he found in a hollow under the roots a goose with feathers of pure gold. He took it up, and went on to an inn, where he proposed to sleep for the night. The landlord had three daughters; and when they saw the goose, they were very curious to examine what this wonderful bird could be, and wished very much to pluck one of the feathers out of its tail.

At last the eldest said, 'I must and will have a feather.' So she waited till his back was turned, and then seized the goose by the wing; but to her great surprise there she stuck, for neither hand nor finger could she get away again. Presently in came the second sister, and thought she would have a feather too; but the moment she touched her sister, there she too hung fast. At last came the third, and wanted a feather; but the other two cried out, 'Keep away! for heaven's sake, keep away!' However, she did not understand what they meant. 'If they are there,' thought she, 'I may as well be there too.' So she went up to them; but the moment she touched her sisters she stuck fast, and hung to the goose as they did. And so they kept company with the goose all night.

The next morning Dummling carried off the goose under his arm; he took no notice of the three girls, but went out with them sticking fast behind; and wherever he travelled, they too were obliged to follow, whether they wanted to or not, as fast as their legs could carry them.

In the middle of a field the parson met them; and when he saw the train, he said, 'Are you not ashamed of yourselves, you bold girls, to run after the young man in that way over the fields? Is that proper behaviour?' Then he took the youngest by the hand to lead her away; but the moment he touched her he too hung fast, and followed in the train.

Presently up came the clerk; and when he saw his master, the parson, running after three girls, he wondered greatly, and said, 'Hello! hello! your reverence! Whither so fast? There is a christening to-day.' Then he ran up, and took him by the gown, and in a moment he was fast too. As the five were thus trudging along, one behind another, they met two labourers with their pickaxes coming from work; and the parson cried out to them to set him free. But scarcely had they touched him, when they too fell into the ranks, and so made seven, all running after Dummling and his goose.

At last they arrived at a city, where reigned a king who had an only daughter. The princess was of so thoughtful and serious a turn of mind that no one could make her laugh; and the king had proclaimed to all the world, that whoever could make her laugh should have her for his wife. When the young man heard this, he went to her with his goose and all its train; and as soon as she saw the seven all hanging together, and running about, treading on each other's heels, she could not help bursting into a long and loud laugh.

Then Dummling claimed her for his wife; the wedding was celebrated, and he was heir to the kingdom, and lived long and happily with his wife.

The Golden Goose *opposite*: When Dummling heard that no one could make the princess laugh, he went to her with his goose and all its train.

Cinderella

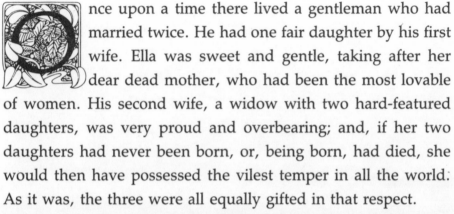

nce upon a time there lived a gentleman who had married twice. He had one fair daughter by his first wife. Ella was sweet and gentle, taking after her dear dead mother, who had been the most lovable of women. His second wife, a widow with two hard-featured daughters, was very proud and overbearing; and, if her two daughters had never been born, or, being born, had died, she would then have possessed the vilest temper in all the world. As it was, the three were all equally gifted in that respect.

From the very day of the wedding the step-mother and her daughters took a violent dislike to the young girl, for they could see how beautiful she was, both outwardly and inwardly; and green envy soon turns to hate. They dared not show it openly, for fear of the father's anger; but he, poor man, finding he had taken too heavy a burden upon his shoulders, fell ill and died – simply worried into his grave. Then his young daughter reaped the full measure of jealousy and spite and malice which her step-mother and sisters could now openly bestow upon her. She was put to do the drudgery of the household with no wages at all, and what was saved in this way was spent on the finery so sorely needed to make the two hard-featured ones at all passable. The poor girl scrubbed the floors, polished the brass,

Cinderella *opposite*: The house was very still. Cinderella, watching the pictures in the glowing embers, could almost hear what the prince of her dreams was saying.

swept the rooms and stairs, cleaned the windows, wrung out the washing and made the beds; and in the evening, when all the work was done, she would sit by the kitchen fire darning the stockings for recreation. When bedtime came she would gaze awhile into the fire, answer the door to her step-sisters coming home from the theatre in all their finery; and then, with their stinging words still in her ears, she would creep up to bed in the garret, there, on a wretched straw mattress, to fall fast asleep from weariness and dream of princes and palaces till at morning light she had to begin her dreary round again.

And it was indeed a dreary round. No sooner had she begun to sift the cinders when the bell would ring, and ring again. One of the sisters wanted her – sometimes both wanted her at once. It was merely a matter of a pin to be fixed, or a ribbon to be tied, but when she came to do it she met with a shower of abuse: 'Look at your hands, you dirty little kitchen slug! How dare you answer the bell with such hands? And your face? Go and look in the mirror, Ella. No, go straight to the kitchen pump – dirty little slug!'

The 'mirror' was quickly changed to the 'kitchen pump' because they knew very well that if she stood before the mirror she would see the reflection of a very beautiful girl – a reflection which they themselves spent hours looking for but could never find.

Yet the child endured it all patiently, and when her work was done, which happened sometimes, she would sit in the chimney corner among the cinders, dreaming of things which no one knows. And it was from this habit of musing among the cinders that she got her name of Cinder-slug which was afterwards softened, for some unknown reason, to Cinderella.

Now the day of a great festival drew near. It was the occasion of the king's son's coming of age, and it was spread abroad that he would select his bride from amongst the most beautiful attending the state ball. As soon as the elder sisters got breath of this they preeked and preened and powdered and anointed, and even ran to the door themselves at every knock, for they expected invitations; and they were not disappointed, for you will easily see that at a ball even beauty must have its plain background to set it off. Very proud they were of their gold-lettered invitation cards bearing the royal seal, and, when they rang for Cinderella, they held them in their hands to emphasise their orders. This must be ironed, just so; this must be pressed and set aside in tissue paper; this must be tucked and frilled and pleated in such a fashion, and so on with crimping and pleating and tabbing and piping and boxing, until poor Cinderella began to wonder why the lot of some was so easy and the lot of others so hard. Nevertheless, she worked and worked and worked; and always in her drudgery came day-dreams of what *she* would wear if she were invited to the ball. She had it all planned out to the smallest frill – but how absurd! She must toil at her sisters' bidding and, on the great night when they were there in their finery, she must sit among the cinders dreaming – in a fairy world of her own – of the prince who came to claim her as his bride. Fool! What a wild fancy! What an unattainable dream! – and there was the bell ringing again: her sisters wanted something, and woe betide her if she dallied, even for a minute.

At last the night of the ball arrived. Early on towards the evening there was no peace in the household. When the elder sister had fully decided in spite of her complexion, to wear her velvet crimson dress trimmed *à l'anglaise*, and the younger had brought out her gold-flowered robe in conjunction with a jewelled stomacher, to say nothing of an old silk underskirt, which, after all, would be hidden; when they had squabbled over the different jewels they possessed, each complimenting the other on the set she desired least herself; when the milliner and the hairdresser had called and gone away exhausted; when the beauty specialist had reached the limit of his art and departed sighing heavily; then, and not till then, was Cinderella called up and allowed the great privilege of admiring the result.

Now Cinderella had, by nature, what one might call 'absolute taste'. She knew instinctively how one should look at a state ball, and she gave them her simple, but perfect, advice, with a deft touch to this and that, which made all the difference. She got no thanks, of course; but one of the sisters did unbend a little.

'Cinderella,' said she, 'wouldn't you like to be going to the ball?'

'Heigho!' sighed Cinderella. 'Such delights are not for me. I dream of them, but that is all.'

'Quite enough, too,' said the other sister. 'Fancy the Cinderslug at a ball! How the whole Court would laugh at such a sorry sight!'

Cinderella made no reply, though the words hurt her. Pin after pin she took from her mouth and fixed it dexterously, where you or I might have done some accidental damage with it, and drawn blood. But not so Cinderella. She had no venom in her nature. When she had arrayed them perfectly she expected no thanks, but just listened to their fault-finding with a hidden smile.

It was only when they had left the house, and she was going downstairs to the kitchen, that one word escaped her: 'Cats!' And if she had not said that she would not have been a girl at all, but only an angel. Then she sat down in her favourite place in the chimney corner to look into the fire and imagine things quite different from what they were. She sat and she dreamed.

The house was very still – so still that you could have heard a pin fall in the top room. The step-mother was on a visit to a maiden aunt, who was not only dying, but very rich, so the best thing to do was to show the dying aunt her invitation card to the ball and play another card – the ace of self-sacrifice. Yes, the house was *very* still. Cinderella, watching the pictures in the glowing embers, could almost hear what the prince of her dreams was saying.

All of a sudden a storm of feeling seemed to burst in her bosom. She – Cinderella – was sitting there alone in the chimney corner dreaming dreams of princes and palaces: what a contrast between what *was* and what *was not*, nor ever could be! All of this was really too much for the child; Cinderella broke down, and, taking her head in her hands, she sobbed as if her heart would break.

While she was still crying bitterly, a gust of cold air swept through the kitchen. She looked up, thinking that the door had blown open. But no, it was shut. Then she gradually became aware of a blue mist gathering and revolving upon itself on the other side of the fireplace. It grew bluer still, and began to shine from within. It spun itself to a standstill, and there, all radiant, stood the strangest little lady you could ever imagine. Her dress was like that of the fairy mother of a prince, with billowy lace flounces and a delicate waist. There was not an inch of it that did not sparkle with a jewel. And as this little lady stood, fingering her wand and looking lovingly and laughingly at Cinderella, the girl knew not what to do. She could only smile back to those kindly eyes, while, half-dazed, she fell to counting the powdered ringlets of her hair, which was so very beautiful that surely it must have been grown in Fairyland! Then, when she looked again at the wand and saw a bright blue flame issue shimmering from the tip of it, Cinderalla was certain that the door of Fairyland had opened and someone very special had stepped out.

'Good evening, my dear,' said the apparition, in the voice and manner of one who could do things. 'Dry your tears and tell me all about it.'

Cinderella was gazing up at her with wonder in her beautiful eyes, though they still brimmed with misery.

'Oh!' she said, choking down her sobs, 'I want, I want – I want to go –' and then she broke down again and could say no more.

'Ah! you got that want from me, I'll warrant; for I have come on purpose to supply it. You want to go to the ball, my dear; that's what you want, though you didn't know it before. And you shall. Come, come, dry your eyes, and we'll see about it. I'm your fairy godmother, you know; and your dear mother, whom I knew very well, has sent me to you. That's better, you've got your mother's smile. Ah! how beautiful she was, to be sure, and you – you're her living image. Now to work! Have you any pumpkins in the garden?'

'What an odd question!' thought Cinderella, although she didn't say anything. 'Why pumpkins? But still, why not?' Then she hastened to assure her fairy godmother that there were plenty of them, big and ripe.

Together they went out into the dark garden, and Cinderella led the way to the pumpkin bed.

'That one there,' said her godmother, pointing with her wand at the finest and largest pumpkin, 'pick it and bring it along with you.'

Cinderella, wondering greatly, obeyed and her godmother led her to the front doorstep, where, bidding the child sit beside her, she took from the bosom of her dress a silver fruit-knife, and with this she scooped out the fruit of the pumpkin, leaving only the rind. This she set down in the street before them, and then touched it with her wand, when – lo and behold! – the pumpkin was immediately transformed into a magnificent coach, all wrought with pure gold. It was the most beautiful thing that she had ever seen.

Cinderella was so amazed that she could not speak. She caught a quick breath of delight, and waited.

'That's that!' said her godmother; 'now for the horses. Let me see: I suppose you haven't a mouse trap anywhere in the house.'

'Yes, yes, I have,' cried Cinderella; 'I set one early this evening, and I always catch such a lot – sometimes a whole family at once.'

'Then go find it, child; we shall want at least six.'

So Cinderella ran in and found the mouse trap she had set; and, sure enough, there was a whole family of six – father and mother, a maiden aunt, and three naughty children who had led them into the trap. In high glee Cinderella ran back to her godmother and showed her.

'Yes, yes; that is quite good, but we're going a bit too fast. Here are six horses – though they don't look it at present – but we must first have a coachman to manage them. Now I don't suppose, by any chance, you've got a –'

'A rat?' cried Cinderella, her eyes sparkling with excitement. 'Well, now, I *did* set a rat trap in the scullery.

'Run, then, and see, child. We can do nothing without a coachman – nothing at all.'

So Cinderella ran to the scullery and fetched the rat trap. In it were three large rats, and the two inspected the rats very closely.

'I think that's the best one,' said Cinderella; 'look at his enormous whiskers! He'd make a lovely coachman.'

'You're right, child; I was just thinking that myself: he's got a good eye for horse-flesh too.'

With this the fairy godmother touched him with the tip of her wand, and instantly he stood before them – a fat coachman with tremendous whiskers, saluting and waiting for orders.

'Now,' said the fairy godmother to Cinderella, 'open the door of the mouse trap and let one out at a time.'

Cinderella did so, and, as each mouse came out, the godmother tapped it with her wand, and it was immediately changed into a magnificent horse, richly harnessed and equipped. The coachman took charge of them and harnessed them to the coach as a six-in-hand.

'That's that!' said the fairy. 'Now for the footmen. Run, child, down to the farther end of the garden. There, in the corner, behind the old broken water-pot, something tells me you will find six lizards in a nest. Gather them up and bring them here to me.'

Cinderella ran off, and soon returned with the identical six lizards. A tap of the wand on each and there stood six imposing footmen, such as are only seen in king's palaces. Their liveries were dazzling with purple and gold. To the manner born they seemed, as they took their places on the magnificent golden coach and waited.

'But – but,' cried Cinderella, who saw by now that she was bound for the ball, 'how can I go like this? They would all jeer at me.'

Her godmother laughed and chided her for having so little faith. 'Tut, tut,' she said, and tapped her on the shoulder with her wand.

What a transformation! The girl, lovely indeed in herself, that stood a moment ago in rags, now stood there a splendid woman – for there is always a moment when a child becomes a woman – and a woman clothed in cloth of gold and silver, all bespangled with jewels. The maids of Fairyland had done her hair up to show its beauty; and in it was fastened a diamond clasp that challenged the sparkling stars. This was topped with a head-dress of finest gossamer.

'But,' said Cinderella, when she had recovered from her amazement, 'I see that I have lovely silk stockings, yet, O my godmother, where are my shoes?'

'Ah! That is just the point.' And her godmother drew from the folds of her dress a pair of glass slippers. 'Glass is glass, I know, my dear; and it is not one in a hundred thousand that could wear such things; but perfect fit is everything, and, as for these, I doubt if there is anyone in the world but yourself who could fit them exactly.'

Cinderella took the slippers and poked her toes into them very carefully, for, as her godmother had said, glass is glass, and you have to be measured very carefully for it. But what was her delight to find that they were, indeed, an absolute fit. Either her feet had been made for the slippers or the slippers had been made for her feet, it did not matter: it was the same thing, and not a little surprising.

Now Cinderella stood up, a perfect picture, and kissed her godmother and thanked her. The carriage was waiting, the horses were restive, the coachman sat on the box, and the footmen were in their places.

'Now, there's just one thing which is rather important,' said the fairy godmother, as Cinderella entered the coach, 'and you must not forget it. I can do this, that, and the other, but at midnight there's an end to it all. You must leave the ball before the clock strikes twelve, for, if you don't, you'll be in a pretty pickle. Your coach will turn into a pumpkin again, your coachman into a rat, your horses into mice, and your footmen into lizards; and there you will be in the ballroom in nothing but your dirty rags for all to laugh at. Now remember: it all ends at the stroke of twelve.'

'Never fear,' said Cinderella. 'I shall not forget. Goodbye!'

'Goodbye, child!'

Then the coachman cracked his whip and the prancing horses sprang forward. Cinderella was off to the ball.

'That's that!' said the fairy godmother, as she looked after the coach for a moment. Then the blue flame at the tip of her wand went out, and so did she – *flick*!

It was a glorious night. The same moon that had looked down on Cinderella's pumpkins now shone upon the king's palace and the royal gardens. Within, the ball was at its height. The movement of the dance was a fascinating spectacle. In the great hall the light of a thousand candles was reflected from the polished floor; from the recesses came the soft splash of cool fountains and the fragrance of the rarest flowers; while, to the sweet strains of the violins, many pairs of feet glided as if on air. Without, among the trees, where hanging lanterns shed a dim light and the music throbbed faintly on the warm night air, couples strayed and lingered, speaking in voices sweet and low, while from cloud to cloud wandered the moon, withdrawing to hide a maiden's blushes, shining forth again to light her smiles.

Suddenly a note of something unusual seemed to run through the whole scene. The chamberlain was seen to speed hither and thither on some quest that left his dignity to see after itself. Breathless he was as he sought the Prince, and at last he found him.

'Your Serene Highness,' he gasped, 'a princess of high degree has just arrived in state and desires admission. She will not give her name, but – if you will permit me to be skilled in these matters – she is a lady that cannot be denied. Beautiful as a goddess and proud as a queen; why, the very jewels in her hair are worth a thousand square miles of territory. Believe me, Your Serene Highness, she is a princess of exalted dignity.'

The Prince followed the chamberlain to the gate, where they found the fair unknown waiting in her coach. The Prince, silent for want of words – she was so very beautiful – handed her down and escorted her through the palace gardens, where, as they passed, the guests started and sighed at sight of one so rare. So they reached the ballroom, and immediately the dance ceased. Even the music fainted away as this vision of beauty came upon the scene. All was at a silent standstill as the Prince led the unknown down the hall, and nothing could be heard but whispers of 'Ah! how beautiful she is!' and 'Never, never have I seen such loveliness!'

Even the old king was altogether fascinated. 'My dear!' he said to the queen in a whisper, 'what an adorable woman! Ah! She and those very words remind me of you yourself.' From which the queen, by a rapid retrospect, inferred that the stranger was indeed a very beautiful woman, and did not hesitate to admit it.

The Prince presented the stranger with few words – for beauty speaks for itself – and then led her out to dance. *Tara tara tara ra ra ra!* – the fiddles struck up a sprightly measure, and all the couples footed it with glee; but one after another they wilted away to watch the graceful pair, so exquisitely did they dance. And then, as if by common consent, the music fell to a dreamy waltz; the Prince and the fair unknown passed into the rhythm, and all were spellbound as this perfect couple danced before them. Even the hard-featured step-sisters were lost in admiration, for little they guessed who the beautiful stranger really was.

The night wore on, and Cinderella danced with the stateliest of the land, and again and again with the Prince. And when supper was over, and the Prince had claimed her for yet another dance, she almost fainted in his arms when she happened to glance at the clock and saw that it was just two minutes to twelve. Alas! Her godmother's warning! She had fallen madly in love with the Prince, as he with her, and she had forgotten everything beside. But now it was a case of quick action or she would soon be in rags and coachless; she could see it so clearly. How they would all laugh at her then!

With a wrench she tore herself away, and, concealing her

haste till she got clear of the ballroom, sped like a deer through the ways of the palace till she reached the marble steps leading down to the gate, when she heard with dismay the ominous sound of a great clock striking twelve.

Down she went three steps at a time, a flying figure of haste in the moonlight. One of her glass slippers came off, but she had to leave it. There – there was the coach waiting for her. She rushed towards it, when, lo and behold, as the last stroke of twelve died away, there was no coach at all; nothing but a hollow pumpkin by the kerb, and six mice and a heavily whiskered rat nibbling at it, to say nothing of six lizards wriggling away. And that was not all. She looked at herself in horror. She was in rags!

With the one thought to hide herself, she ran as fast as her legs would carry her in the direction of her home. She had scarcely covered half the distance when it came on to rain hard, and before she reached her doorstep, she was drenched to the skin. Then, when she had crept to her chimney corner in the kitchen, she made a strange discovery. As you know, the coach and all that appertained to it had disappeared; her splendid attire had gone; but – how was this? – one real glass slipper still remained. The other, she remembered, she had dropped on the steps of the palace.

'Well, child?' said a clear voice from the other side of the fireplace; and Cinderella looking up, saw her godmother standing there gazing down at her with a wise but quizzical smile.

'The slippers! she went on. 'Oh no; however forgetful you might have been, they could never have vanished like the other things. Don't you remember, I brought them with me? They were *real*. But where is the other one?'

'In my haste to get away I dropped it on the palace steps.' And Cinderella began to cry.

'There, there; never mind. You were certainly very careless, but you are not unlucky – at least, not if I can help it.' And when Cinderella looked up through her tears her godmother had gone.

Cinderella sat musing as she gazed into the dying fire. But just then the bell rang announcing the return of her step-sisters. Oh! they were full of it! A most beautiful princess had been to the ball, they said, and they had actually spoken with her. She was most gentle and condescending. Their faces shone with reflected glory. And she had left suddenly at midnight, and the Prince was beside himself; and there was nothing to show for it all but a glass slipper which he had picked up on the steps of the palace. What a night! And so they rambled on, little thinking that Cinderella had the other glass slipper hidden in her bosom along with other secrets.

The next day events followed one another with great rapidity. First, came a royal proclamation. Whereas a lady had lost a slipper at the ball it must be returned to the rightful owner, and so forth. Secondly, came news that the slipper had been tried on the princesses, duchesses, marchionesses, countesses, and viscountesses, and finally on the baronesses of the Court, but all in vain. It fitted none of them. Thirdly, it gradually became known that any lady with a foot that betokened good breeding was invited to call at the palace and try on the slipper. This went on for weeks, and finally the prime minister, who carried the glass slipper on a velvet cushion, went out himself to search for the fitting foot, for the Prince was leading him a dog's life, and threatening all kinds of things unless that foot and all that was joined to it were found.

At last, going from house to house, he came to Cinderella's sisters, who, of course, tried all they could to squeeze a foot into the slipper, but without success. Cinderella looked on and laughed to herself to see how hard they tried, and, when they had given it up, she said gaily, 'Let me try and see if I can get it on.'

Her sisters laughed loudly at the idea of a little kitchen slug like Cinderella trying her luck, and both of them began to mock and abuse her; but the chamberlain, seeing what a beautiful girl she was, maintained that his orders were to try it upon everyone.

So Cinderella held out her little foot, and the chamberlain put the slipper on quite easily. It fitted like wax. This was an astonishing thing, but it was more astonishing still when Cinderella produced the other slipper and put it on the other foot. Then, to show that wonders would never cease, the door flew open, and in came the fairy godmother. Quick as a flash, with one touch of her wand on Cinderella's clothes, there she stood again dressed as on the night of the ball, only this time there were not only jewels in her hair but beautifully scented orange blossoms as well.

There was a breathless silence for a while. Then, when Cinderella's step-sisters realised that she was the same beautiful unknown that they had seen at the ball, they prostrated themselves before her, begging her to forgive all. Cinderella took them by the hand and raised them up and kissed them. And it melted their hard natures to hear her say that she would love them always.

When the fairy godmother had witnessed all this she said to herself, 'That's that!' and vanished. But she never lost sight of Cinderella. She guided and guarded her in all her ways, and, when the Prince claimed his willing bride, their way of happiness was strewn with roses.

Cinderella *opposite*: What a transformation! The girl, lovely indeed in herself, that stood a moment ago in her rags, now stood there a splendid woman clothed in cloth of gold and silver.

Cinderella *page 102*: So Cinderella held out her little foot, and the chamberlain put the slipper on quite easily. It fitted like wax. It was more astonishing still when Cinderella produced the other slipper.

The Three Little Pigs

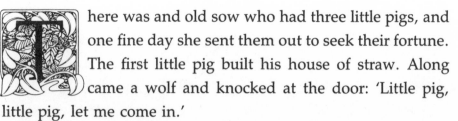

here was and old sow who had three little pigs, and one fine day she sent them out to seek their fortune. The first little pig built his house of straw. Along came a wolf and knocked at the door: 'Little pig, little pig, let me come in.'

The pig answered, 'Not by the hair of my chiny chin chin.'

'Then I'll huff, and I'll puff, and I'll blow your house in.' He huffed, and he puffed, and he blew the house in, and ate up the pig.

The second little pig built his house of sticks. Along came the wolf: 'Little pig, little pig, let me come in.'

'No, no, not by the hair of my chiny chin chin.'

'Then I'll huff, and I'll puff, and I'll blow your house in.' He huffed and he puffed and he blew the house in, and ate the pig.

The third little pig built his house of bricks. The wolf knocked at the door: 'Little pig, little pig, let me come in.'

'No, no, not by the hair of my chiny chin chin.'

'Then I'll huff, and I'll puff, and I'll blow your house in.' So he huffed and he puffed, but he could not blow the house in. He decided to trick the little pig another way: 'Little pig, I know where there is a field of turnips.'

'Where?' asked the little pig.

'Oh, in Mr. Smith's field; if you will be ready tomorrow morning I will call for you, and we will get some for dinner.'

'Very well,' said the little pig, 'What time do you mean to go?'

'Oh, at six o'clock,' said the wolf.

Well, the little pig woke up at five, and got the turnips before the wolf came, who said: 'Little pig, are you ready?'

The little pig said: 'I went and got a potful for dinner.'

The wolf felt very angry at this, but he didn't give up: 'Little pig, there is a fair this afternoon, will you go?'

'Oh yes,' said the pig, 'What time shall you be ready?'

'At three,' said the wolf.

So the little pig went off to the fair early, and bought a butter-churn. He was going home when he saw the wolf coming. He didn't know what to do. So he hid in the churn, and by so doing turned it round. It rolled down the hill with the pig in it, which frightened the wolf and he ran home. He went to the little pig's house, and told him how frightened he had been by a great round thing which came down the hill past him. The little pig said: 'Hah, I frightened you! I went to the fair and bought a butter-churn. When I saw you, I got into it, and rolled down the hill.'

The wolf was very angry, and declared he *would* eat up the little pig, and he began to climb down the chimney. When the little pig saw what he was doing, he hung a pot full of water over a blazing fire. Just as the wolf was coming down, he took off the cover, and in fell the wolf. The little pig put on the cover, boiled him up, ate him for supper, and lived happily ever after.

Little Goody Two-Shoes

ll the world must allow that Two-shoes was not her real name. No, her father's name was Meanwell and he was for many years a well-to-do farmer in the village where Margery was born. The Meanwells were a happy family and Margery and her little brother Tommy enjoyed living on the farm. But bad times came, another farmer, Mr. Graspall cheated Farmer Meanwell out of his farm and shortly afterwards the poor man died of a fever. Margery's mother was heartbroken and a few days later she died too. The children were very sad for they now had neither father nor mother and their rich relatives took no notice of them.

Margery and little Tommy loved each other dearly. Hand in hand they trotted about, their clothes becoming more and more ragged, and, although Tommy had two shoes, Margery had only one. The poor little things had nothing to eat but what they picked from the hedges or were given by poor people. Each night they slept in a barn and comforted each other.

Then Mr. Smith, a clergyman in the village, heard about their plight from a good old gentleman who had seen the two ragged and hungry children, and he sent for them. The kind old gentleman ordered a new pair of shoes to be made for little Margery, and gave Mr. and Mrs. Smith money to buy her some new clothes. He himself offered to take Tommy and have him trained as a sailor. So at last the children had a home with food to eat and clothes to keep them warm.

A few days later the old gentleman decided to go to London, taking Tommy with him. Both the children cried and kissed each other a hundred times, for this was the first time in their lives they were to be parted. At last Tommy wiped away Margery's tears with the end of his jacket and said he would come and find her when he returned from sea. Margery went to bed that night crying and when she woke up next morning, Tommy was gone. Little Margery ran all round the village crying for her brother and returned to the Smiths' house very sadly when she couldn't find him.

Fortunately, at this moment the shoemaker came along with her new shoes. Margery was very excited to have two new shoes and took great pleasure in them. She ran to Mrs. Smith as soon as they were put on, calling out, 'Two shoes, see two shoes.' And she did the same to all the people she met. And this is how she got the name Little Goody Two-shoes.

Little Margery was very happy living with Mr. and Mrs. Smith, who had agreed to bring her up with their own children. Then the wicked Mr. Graspall, who had ruined her father, heard where she was living and he threatened to ruin Mr. Smith too if he kept Margery. So Mr. and Mrs. Smith, crying and kissing her, were obliged to send her away.

Poor Margery made her way sadly to another village some distance away where, once again, the only shelter she could find was in a barn. But she always remembered how good and wise Mr. Smith was, and she decided that this was because of his great learning. More than anything in the world she wanted to learn how to read, so she would wait for the boys and girls as they came from school and would borrow their books. She soon knew more than any of her playmates and decided to teach those who had no opportunity to go to school. She knew that only twenty-six letters were required to spell all the words we ever need. As some of these letters are large and some are small, she, with her knife, cut out of several pieces of wood ten sets of each of the small ones and six sets of each of the large ones.

Every morning she used to go round with the wooden letters in a basket to teach the children. First she went to Farmer Wilson's. Here Margery stopped, and ran up to the door, giving a tap.

'Who's there?'

'Only Little Goody Two-shoes,' answers Margery. 'I've come to teach Billy.'

'Oh, Little Goody,' says Mrs. Wilson. 'I am glad you've come. Billy wants to see you badly for he has learned all his lessons.'

Then out came the little boy, 'How do doody Two-shoes?' says he, not being able to speak very clearly. Yet he had learned all his letters, for when Little Goody Two-shoes threw down all the letters of the alphabet mixed up together, he picked them up, called them by their right names and put them in order.

The next place she came to was Gaffer Cook's cottage. Here some poor children met to learn. They all came round little Margery at once. Having pulled out her letters, she asked the boy next to her what he had eaten for dinner.

He answered, 'Bread.' Indeed they were so poor that they lived on very little else.

'Well then,' says she, 'put the first letter down there.'

He then put down the letter *B*, to which he next added *r*, and the next *e*, the next *a*, the next *d*, and it stood thus: *Bread*.

'And what had you, Polly Comb, for your dinner?' asked little Margery.

'Apple-pie,' answered the little girl; and so the lessons went on in this way.

The next place she went to was Farmer Thompson's, where there were a good many little ones waiting for her. They all huddled round her, and – though at the other place they were concerned with words and syllables – here were children of much greater ability, who dealt in sentences, which they set up and read aloud.

Eventually it came about that Mrs. Williams, who kept a little school in the neighbourhood, became very old and infirm, and it was decided that Margery should take up her work. From that moment she was known as Mrs. Margery.

One day Mrs. Margery brought home a fine young raven which she had rescued from some village boys who were tormenting it. Now, this bird, which she called Ralph, she taught to speak, to spell, and to read. He sat at her elbow, and when any of the children were wrong she used to call out, 'Put them right Ralph.'

This sensible bird composed a rhyme which all the children learned by heart: 'Early to bed and early to rise is the way to be healthy, wealthy and wise.'

She had also a pigeon, which she rescued from the same naughty boys. Like the raven, she taught this bird to spell and read, though not to talk. He was a very pretty fellow and she called him Tom.

Then the neighbours, knowing that Mrs. Margery liked animals, made her a present of a little dog. She called him Jumper because he was always jumping and playing about. Jumper was gate-keeper of the school; he would let nobody go out or come in without the permission of his mistress.

One Thursday morning Jumper all of a sudden caught hold of his mistress's apron, and tried to pull her out of the school. She was at first surprised, but she followed him to see what it was he wanted of her.

No sooner had he led her into the garden than he ran back and pulled out one of the children in the same manner; upon which she ordered them all to leave the school immediately, and they had not been out five minutes before the roof of the house fell in.

The downfall of the school was a great misfortune for Mrs. Margery, for she not only lost all her books but was without a place to teach in. Soon afterwards, however, one of the local landowners had the school rebuilt for her.

Mrs. Margery was always helping her neighbours in all kinds of ways and she was very popular in the village. One gentleman, Sir Charles Jones, had come to hold such a high opinion of her that he offered her a lot of money to take care of his family and teach his daughter, which, however, she refused.

Some time later, Sir Charles became dangerously ill and Mrs. Margery hastened to his house to look after him. She nursed him so well that he fell in love with her and asked her to marry him.

The wedding day arrived and the church was filled with all the neighbours who had come to wish Mrs. Margery well. But just as the clergyman had opened his book to begin the service a gentleman ran into the church and cried out, 'Stop! Stop!'

At first the congregation was alarmed, but the alarm turned to delight when it became known that this gentleman was Mrs. Margery's brother, who had just returned from overseas where he had made a large fortune. On coming to look for his sister he heard of her intended wedding and had ridden in great haste to arrange a proper dowry for her, as he was now able to give her an ample fortune.

Mrs. Margery, or Lady Jones as she became after her marriage, still went on with her good works. She was a mother to the poor, a doctor to the sick, and a friend to all in distress and she was loved by everybody.

But what of Mr. Smith and Mr. Graspall? Mr. Smith – the man who had been so kind to Little Goody Two-Shoes such a long time ago – finally took Mr. Graspall to court, for he had been cheating people all those years. Mr. Smith won the case. Lady Jones bought the whole estate and made it into little farms that could never again be dominated by a wicked man. And of course she always took good care of her dear old friends, Mr. and Mrs. Smith.

Little Goody Two-Shoes *opposite*: At this moment the shoemaker came along with her new shoes. Margery went to Mrs. Smith as soon as they were put on, calling out, 'Two shoes, see two shoes!'

The Babes in the Wood

Once upon a time two children lived in a big house on the borders of a wood. Their parents, who loved them very dearly, were rich enough to buy them all the lovely things they longed for, and all day long they played in a beautiful garden, learning the songs of the birds and the secrets of the flowers. But one sad day their father and mother left them for a happier home in heaven, and the sister and brother were left alone.

The boy did his best to comfort his little sister; but they were sad days, and though they did not know it then, days that were sadder still were soon to come.

The children had an uncle whom they had never seen. He lived far away across the seas; but as soon as he learned of the death of his brother, the children's father, he hurried to their home. He knew that now their father was dead the children would have all his money, and the uncle also knew that if he could get rid of the children all this money would be his.

And the more he thought about this money the more he longed for it. And then a dreadful thought came into his head. He determined to kill the little innocent children and take their money.

So he hired two robbers, and paid them to take the children

The Babes in the Wood *opposite*: The children were left all alone in the wood. They dared not return to their wicked uncle, so they wandered on, hand in hand, hoping to find shelter.

to a lonely spot in the wood and there kill them.

One morning, when the sun shone brightly and all the birds were gay, the robbers crept into the garden where the children were playing and took them away. The robbers were big, rough men, and the children were afraid; but the men told the children that their uncle had sent them, and they dared not disobey.

The men led them out of the garden into the wood, and on and on till they came to a deserted spot. They had come a long way, and the children were glad to rest. They sat down on the trunk of a tree while the robbers moved away and carried on a conversation in a low voice. Presently they began to quarrel; their voices became loud and angry, and the children heard words that made them tremble with fear.

'I've been paid to kill them, and I shall earn my money,' one of them was saying, over and over again.

But the other robber seemed to feel more kindly toward the children. 'Why kill them?' he said. 'Let us lose them, and perhaps someone may find them and give them shelter.'

The little girl crept closer to her brother. 'They want to kill us,' she said, in a terrified whisper.

But before the boy could answer, the kindly robber, leaving his companion, came forward and spoke to them. 'Stay here while we go to find food and shelter for the night,' he said gruffly.

Then they went away, and the children were left all alone in the wood. They dared not return to their wicked uncle, and they had no other home; so they wandered on, hand in hand, hoping to find shelter.

The forest was very beautiful, and for a time they were happy among the wild flowers and ferns; but soon the sun went down, the birds hushed their songs, and a great stillness came over all. Yet the children toiled bravely on, tired, and hungry, and sad.

Presently the trees grew so thickly together that they could scarcely find their way, and at last the darkness of night came on and hid even the trees from sight. Too weary and frightened to go any farther, the children sat down under a friendly oak, and fell asleep in one another's arms.

The birds of the forest peeped down from their nests above; the shy squirrels with their long tails glanced wonderingly at them; then the birds collected the leaves, one by one, and gently placed them on the sleeping children, making a cloak of crimson and gold to cover them.

And when the morning came a beautiful angel flew down and carried them away to their father and mother in the glorious world above, where they were happy once again.

Jack The Giant-Killer

In the reign of good King Arthur, there lived near the Land's End of England, in the county of Cornwall, a farmer who had only one son, called Jack. He was brisk and of a ready lively wit, so that nobody or nothing could get the better of him.

In those days the Mount of Cornwall was kept by a huge giant named Cormoran. He was eighteen feet in height, and about three yards round the waist, of a fierce and grim countenance, the terror of all the neighbouring towns and villages. He lived in a cave in the midst of the Mount, and whenever he wanted food he would wade over to the mainland, where he would furnish himself with whatever came his way. Everybody at his approach ran out of their houses, while he seized on their cattle, making nothing of carrying half a dozen oxen on his back at a time; and as for their sheep and hogs, he would tie them round his waist like a bunch of tallow-dips. He had done this for many years, so that all Cornwall was in despair.

One day Jack happened to be at the Town Hall when the magistrates were sitting in council about the Giant. He asked: 'What reward will be given to the man who kills Cormoran?'

'The giant's treasure,' they said, 'will be the reward.'

Quoth Jack: 'Then let me undertake it?'

So he got a horn, shovel, and pickaxe, and went over to the Mount early on a dark winter's evening, when he fell to work, and before morning had dug a pit twenty-two feet deep, and nearly as broad, covering it over with long sticks and straw. Then he strewed a little earth over it, so that it appeared like plain ground. Jack then placed himself on the opposite side of the pit, farthest from the giant's lodging, and, just at the break of day, he put the horn to his mouth and blew, *Tantivy, Tantivy.*

This noise roused the giant, who rushed from his cave crying: 'You incorrigible villain, are you come here to disturb my rest? You shall pay dearly for this. Satisfaction I will have, and this it shall be: I will take you whole and broil you for breakfast.' He had no sooner uttered this than he tumbled into the pit and made the very foundations of the Mount shake.

'Oh, Giant,' quoth Jack, 'where are you now? Oh faith, you are gotten now into trouble, where I will surely plague you for your threatening words: what do you think now of broiling me for your breakfast? Will no other diet serve you but poor Jack?' Then, having tantalized the giant for a while, he gave him a most weighty knock with his pickaxe on the very crown of his head and killed him on the spot.

Jack then filled up the pit with earth, and went to search the cave, which he found contained much treasure. When the magistrates heard of this they made a declaration he should henceforth be known as 'Jack the Giant-killer' and presented him with a sword and a belt, on which were written these words, embroidered in letters of gold:

'Here's the right valiant Cornish man
Who slew the giant Cormoran.'

The news of Jack's victory soon spread over all the West of England, so that another giant, named Blunderbore, hearing of it, vowed to be revenged on Jack if ever he should light on him.

This giant was the lord of an enchanted castle situated in the midst of a lonesome wood. Now Jack, about four months afterwards, walking near this wood in his journey to Wales, being weary, seated himself near a pleasant fountain and fell fast asleep. While he was sleeping, the giant, coming there for water, discovered him, and knew him to be the far-famed Jack the Giant-killer by the lines written on his belt. Without ado, he took Jack on his shoulders and carried him towards his castle. Now, as they passed through a thicket, the rustling of the boughs awakened Jack, who was strangely surprised to find himself in the clutches of the giant. His terror was only begun, for, on entering the castle, he saw the ground strewed with human bones, and the giant told him his own would before long be among them. After this the giant locked poor Jack in an immense chamber, leaving him there while he went to fetch another giant, his brother, living in the same wood, who might share in the meal on Jack.

After waiting some time, Jack, on going to the window, beheld afar off the two giants coming towards the castle. 'Now,' quoth Jack to himself, 'my death or my deliverance is at hand.' There were strong cords in a corner of the room in which Jack was, and two of these he took, and made a firm noose at the end; and while the giants were unlocking the iron gate of the castle he threw the ropes over each of their heads. Then he drew the other ends across a beam, and pulled with all his might, so that he throttled them. Then, when he saw they were black in the face, he slid down one of the ropes and, drawing his sword, slew them both. Then, taking the giant's keys and unlocking the rooms, he found three fair ladies tied by the hair of their heads, almost starved to death.

'Sweet ladies,' quoth Jack, 'I have destroyed this monster and his brutish brother, and obtained your liberties.' This said he presented them with the keys, and so proceeded on his journey to Wales.

Jack made the best of his way by travelling as fast as he could, but lost his road, and was overtaken by darkness. He could find no habitation until, coming into a narrow valley, he found a large house, and in order to get shelter took courage to knock at the gate. But what was his surprise when there came forth a monstrous giant with two heads! Yet he did not appear so fiery as the others, for he was a Welsh giant, and what harm he did was by private and secret malice under the false show of friendship. Jack, having told his condition to the giant, was shown into a bedroom, where, in the dead of night, he heard his host in another apartment muttering these words:

'Though here you lodge with me this night,
You shall not see the morning light:
My club shall dash your brains outright!'

'Say'st thou so?' quoth Jack; 'that is like one of your Welsh tricks, yet I hope to be cunning enough for you.' Then, getting out of bed, he laid a billet in the bed in his stead, and hid himself in a corner of the room. In the dead of night in came the Welsh giant, who struck several heavy blows on the bed with his club, thinking he had broken every bone in Jack's skin.

The next morning Jack, laughing in his sleeve, gave him hearty thanks for his night's lodging.

'How have you rested?' quoth the giant; 'did you not feel anything in the night?'

'No,' quoth Jack, 'nothing but a rat, which, silly thing, gave me two or three slaps with her tail.'

With that, greatly wondering, the giant led Jack to breakfast, bringing him a bowl containing four gallons of hasty pudding. Being loath to let the giant think it too much for him, Jack put a large leather bag under his loose coat in such a way that he could convey the pudding into it without it being perceived. Then, telling the giant he would show him a trick, Jack took a knife, ripped open the bag, and out came all the hasty pudding.

Whereupon, saying, 'odds splutters hur nails, hur can do that trick hurself,' the monster took the knife, and ripping open his own belly, fell down dead.

Now it happened in these days that King Arthur's only son asked his father to give him a large sum of money, in order that he might go and seek his fortune in the principality of Wales, where lived a beautiful lady possessed with seven evil spirits. The king did his best to dissuade his son from it, but in vain; so at last he gave way and the prince set out with two horses, one loaded with money, the other for himself to ride upon.

After several days' travel he came to a market-town in Wales, where he beheld a vast crowd of people gathered together. The prince asked the reason of it, and was told that they had arrested a corpse for several large sums of money which the deceased owed when he died.

The prince replied that it was a pity creditors should be so cruel, and said: 'Go bury the dead, and let his creditors come to my lodging, and there their debts shall be paid.' They came in such great numbers that before night he had only twopence left for himself.

Now Jack the Giant-killer, coming that way, was so taken with the generosity of the prince that he desired to be his servant. This being agreed upon, the next morning they set forward on their journey together, when, as they were riding out of the town, an old woman called after the prince, saying: 'He has owed me twopence these seven years; pray pay me as well as the rest.' Putting his hand in his pocket, the prince gave the woman all he had left, so that after their day's food, which cost what small store Jack had by him, they were without a penny between them.

When the sun got low, the king's son said: 'Jack, since we have no money, where can we lodge this night?'

But Jack replied: 'Master, we'll do well enough, for I have an uncle lives within two miles of this place; he is a huge and monstrous giant with three heads. He'll fight five hundred men in armour, and make them to fly before him.'

'Alas!' quoth the prince, 'what shall we do there? He'll certainly chop us up in a mouthful. Nay, we are scarce enough to fill one of his hollow teeth!'

'It is no matter for that,' quoth Jack; 'I myself will go before and prepare the way for you; therefore stop here and wait till I return.' Jack then rode away at full speed, and coming to the gate of the castle, he knocked so loud that he made the neighbouring hills resound.

At this the giant roared out like thunder: 'Who's there?'

Jack answered: 'None but your poor cousin Jack.'

Quoth he: 'What news with my poor cousin Jack?'

He replied: 'Dear uncle, heavy news!'

'Prithee,' quoth the giant, 'what heavy news can come to me? Thou knowest I am a giant with three heads, and besides thou knowest I can fight five hundred men in armour, and make them fly like the very chaff before the wind.'

'Oh, but,' quoth Jack, 'here's the king's son a-coming with a thousand men in armour to kill you and destroy all that you have!'

'Oh, cousin Jack,' said the giant, 'this is heavy news indeed! I will immediately run and hide myself, and thou shalt lock, bolt, and bar me in, and keep the keys until the prince is gone.'

Having secured the giant, Jack fetched his master, when they made themselves heartily merry whilst the poor giant lay trembling in a vault under the ground.

Early in the morning Jack furnished his master with a fresh supply of gold and silver, and then sent him three miles forward on his journey, by which time the prince was pretty well out of the smell of the giant. Jack then returned, and let the giant out of the vault, who asked what he should give him for keeping the castle from destruction.

'Why,' quoth Jack, 'I want nothing but the old coat and cap, together with the old rusty sword and slippers which are at your bed's head.'

Quoth the giant: 'You know not what you ask; they are the most precious things I have. The coat will keep you invisible, the cap will tell you all you want to know, the sword cuts asunder whatever you strike, and the shoes are of extraordinary swiftness. But you have been very serviceable to me, therefore take them with all my heart.'

Jack thanked his uncle, and then went off with them. He soon overtook his master and they quickly arrived at the house of the lady the prince sought, who, finding the prince to be a suitor, prepared a splendid banquet for him.

After the repast was concluded, she told him she had a task for him. She wiped his mouth with a handkerchief, saying: 'You must show me that handkerchief to-morrow morning, or else you will lose your head.' With that she put it in her bosom.

The prince went to bed in great sorrow, but Jack's cap of knowledge informed him how it was to be obtained. In the middle of the night she called upon her familiar spirit to carry her to Lucifer. But Jack put on his coat of darkness and his shoes of swiftness, and was there as soon as she was. When she entered the place of the demon, she gave the handkerchief to him, and he laid it upon a shelf, whence Jack took it and brought it to his master, who showed it to the lady next day, and so saved his life.

On that day she gave the prince a kiss and told him he must show her the lips to-morrow morning that she kissed that night, or lose his head.

'Ah!' he replied, 'if you kiss none but mine, I will.'

'That is neither here nor there,' said she; 'if you do not, death's your portion!'

At midnight she went as before, and was angry with the demon for letting the handkerchief go. 'But now,' quoth she, 'I will be too hard for the king's son for I will kiss thee, and he is to show me thy lips.' Which she did, and Jack, when she was not standing by, cut off Lucifer's head and brought it under his invisible coat to his master, who the next morning pulled it out by the horns before the lady.

This broke the enchantment and the evil spirit left her and she appeared in all her beauty. They were married the next morning and soon after went to the court of King Arthur, where Jack, for his many great exploits, was made one of the Knights of the Round Table.

Jack soon went searching for giants again, but he had not

ridden far when he saw a cave, near the entrance of which he beheld a giant sitting upon a block of timber, with a knotted iron club by his side. His goggle eyes were like flames of fire, his countenance grim and ugly, and his cheeks like a couple of large sides of bacon, while the bristles of his beard resembled rods of iron wire, and the locks that hung down upon his brawny shoulders were like curled snakes or hissing adders.

Jack alighted from his horse, and, putting on the coat of darkness, went up close to the giant, and said softly: 'Oh! Are you there? It will not be long before I take you fast by the beard.' The giant all this while could not see him, on account of his invisible coat, so that Jack, coming up close to the monster, struck a blow with his sword at his head, but, mising his aim, he cut off the nose instead. At this the giant roared like claps of thunder, and began to swing his iron club about him like one stark mad. But Jack, running behind, drove his sword up to the hilt in the giant's back, so that he fell down dead. This done, Jack cut off the giant's head, and sent it, with his brother's also, to King Arthur, by a wagoner he hired for that purpose.

Jack now resolved to enter the giant's cave in search of his treasure, and, passing along through a great many windings and turnings, he came at length to a large room paved with freestone, at the upper end of which was a boiling cauldron, and on the right hand a large table, at which the giant used to dine.

Then he came to a window, barred with iron, through which he looked and beheld a vast number of miserable captives, who, seeing him, cried out: 'Alas! young man, art thou come to be one amongst us in this miserable den?'

'Ay,' quoth Jack, 'but what is the meaning of your captivity?'

'We are kept here,' said one, 'till such time as the giants have a wish to feast, and then the fattest among us is slaughtered! And many are the times they have dined upon murdered men!'

'Say you so?' quoth Jack, and straightway unlocked the gate and let them free, and they all rejoiced like condemned men at sight of a pardon. Then searching the giant's coffers, he shared the gold and silver equally amongst them and took them to a neighbouring castle where they all feasted and made merry.

But in the midst of all this mirth a messenger brought news that one Thunderell, a giant with two heads, having heard of the death of his kinsmen, had come from the northern dales to be revenged on Jack, and was within a mile of the castle, the country people flying before him like chaff.

But Jack was not a bit daunted and said: 'Let him come! I have a tool to pick his teeth; and you, ladies and gentlemen, walk out into the garden, and you shall witness this giant Thunderell's death and destruction.'

The castle was situated in the midst of a small island surrounded by a moat thirty feet deep and twenty feet wide, over which lay a drawbridge. So Jack employed men to cut through this bridge on both sides, nearly to the middle; and then, dressing himself in his invisible coat, he marched against the giant with his sword of sharpness. Although the giant could not see Jack, he smelt his approach.

'Fee, fi, fo, fum!
I smell the blood of an Englishman!
Be he alive or be he dead,
I'll grind his bones to make me bread!'

'Say'st thou so?' said Jack; 'then thou art a monstrous miller.'

The giant cried out again: 'Art thou that villain who killed my kinsmen? Then I will tear thee with my teeth, suck thy blood, and grind thy bones to powder.'

'You'll have to catch me first,' quoth Jack, and throwing off his invisible coat, so that the giant might see him, and putting on his shoes of swiftness, he ran from the giant, who followed like a walking castle, so that the very foundations of the earth seemed to shake at every step. Jack led him a long dance, in order that the gentleman and ladies might see; and at last, to end the matter, ran lightly over the drawbridge, the giant, in full speed, pursuing him with his club.

Then, coming to the middle of the bridge, the giant's great weight broke it down, and he tumbled headlong into the water, where he rolled and wallowed like a whale. Jack, standing by the moat, laughed at him all the while; but though the giant foamed to hear him scoff, and plunged from place to place in the moat, yet he could not get out to be revenged. Jack at length got a cart-rope and cast it over the two heads of the giant, and drew him ashore by a team of horses, and then cut off both his heads with his sword of sharpness and sent them to King Arthur.

After some time spent in mirth and pastime, Jack, taking leave of the knights and ladies, set out for new adventures. Through many woods he passed, and came at length to the foot of a high mountain. Here, late at night, he found a lonesome house, and knocked at the door, which was opened by an aged man with a head of hair as white as snow.

'Father,' said Jack, 'will you be so kind as to lodge a traveller that has lost his way in the dark and needs a place to sleep for the night?'

'Yes,' said the old man; 'you are right welcome to my poor cottage.' Whereupon Jack entered, and down they sat together, and the old man began to speak as follows: 'Son, I see by your belt you are the great conqueror of giants, and behold, my son, on the top of this mountain be an enchanted castle; this is kept by a giant named Galligantua, and he, by the help of an old conjurer, tricks many knights and ladies into his castle, where by magic art they are transformed into sundry shapes and forms. But above all, I grieve for a duke's daughter whom they fetched from her father's garden, carrying her through the air in a burning chariot drawn by fiery dragons. Then they secured her within the castle, and transformed her into a white hind. And though many knights have tried to break the enchantment and work her deliverance, yet no one could accomplish it, on account of two dreadful griffins which are placed at the castle gate and which destroy every one who comes near. But you, my son, may pass by them undiscovered, where on the gates of the castle you will find engraven in large letters how the spell may be broken.'

Jack gave the old man his hand, and promised that in the morning of the very next day he would venture his life to free the lady.

In the morning Jack arose and put on his invisible coat and magic cap and shoes, and prepared himself for the fray. Now when he had reached the top of the mountain he soon discovered the two fiery griffins, but passed them without fear, because of his invisible coat. When he had got beyond them, he found upon the gates of the castle a golden trumpet hung by a silver chain, under which the following lines were clearly engraved:

Whoever shall this trumpet blow
Shall soon the giant overthrow
And break the black enchantment straight
So all shall be in happy state.

Jack had no sooner read this than he blew the trumpet, at which the castle trembled to its vast foundations, and the giant and conjurer were in horrid confusion, biting their thumbs and tearing their hair, knowing their wicked reign was at an end. Then, the giant stooping to take up his club, Jack at one blow cut off his head; whereupon the conjurer, mounting up into the air, was carried away in a whirlwind.

Then the enchantment was broken, and all the lords and ladies who had so long been transformed into birds and beasts returned to their proper shapes, and the castle vanished away in a cloud of smoke. This being done, the head of Galligantua was likewise, in the usual manner, conveyed to the Court of King Arthur, where, the very next day, Jack followed, with the knights and ladies who had been delivered. Whereupon, as a reward for his good services, the king prevailed upon the duke to bestow his daughter in marriage on honest Jack. So married they were, and the whole kingdom was filled with joy at the wedding. Furthermore, the king bestowed on Jack a noble castle, with a very beautiful estate thereto belonging, where he and his lady lived in great joy and happiness all the rest of their days.

Jack the Giant-Killer *opposite*: The Giant said, 'I will take you whole and broil you for breakfast.' No sooner had he uttered this than he tumbled into the pit and made the very foundations of the Mount shake.

Jack the
Giant killer.

Dick Whittington entrusts his cat to the Captain

Dick Whittington

n the reign of the famous King Edward III there was a little boy called Dick Whittington, whose father and mother had died when he was very young. As poor Dick was not old enough to work, he was very badly off; he got but little for his dinner, and sometimes nothing at all for his breakfast; for the people who lived in the village were very poor indeed, and could not spare him much more than the parings of potatoes, and now and then a hard crust of bread.

Now Dick had heard many very strange things about the great city called London; for the country people at that time thought that folks in London were all fine gentlemen and ladies; and that there was singing and music there all day long; and that the streets were all paved with gold.

One day a large wagon and eight horses, all with bells at their heads, drove through the village while Dick was standing by the signpost. He thought that this wagon must be going to the fine town of London; so he took courage, and asked the wagoner to let him walk with him by the side of the wagon. As soon as the wagoner heard that poor Dick had no father or mother, and saw by his ragged clothes that he could not be worse off than he was, he told him he could go if he wanted to, so off they set

Dick Whittington and his Cat *opposite*: Dick brought down poor puss, and gave her to the captain.

on the road to London with each other for company.

So Dick arrived safely in London, and was in such a hurry to see the fine streets paved all over with gold, that he did not even stay to thank the kind wagoner, but ran off as fast as his legs would carry him through many of the streets, thinking every moment to come to those that were paved with gold; for Dick had seen a guinea three times in his own little village, and remembered what a great deal of money it had brought in change. He thought he would have nothing to do but to take up some little bits of the pavement, and would then have as much money as he could wish for.

Poor Dick ran till he was tired, and had quite forgot his friend the wagoner; but at last, finding it growing dark, and that every way he turned he saw nothing but dirt instead of gold, he sat down in a dark corner and cried himself to sleep.

Little Dick was all night in the street; and next morning, being very hungry, he got up and walked about, and asked everybody he met to give him a halfpenny to keep him from starving; but nobody stayed to answer him, and only two or three gave him a halfpenny, so that the poor boy was soon quite weak and faint for the want of victuals.

In this distress he asked charity of several people, and one of them said crossly: 'Go to work, you idle rogue.'

'That I will,' says Dick, 'I will to go work for you, if you will let me.' But the man only cursed at him and went on.

At last a good-natured-looking gentleman saw how hungry he looked. 'Why don't you go to work my lad?' said he to Dick.

'That I would, but I do not know how to get any,' answered Dick.

'If you are willing, come along with me,' said the gentlemen, and took him to a hay-field, where Dick worked briskly, and lived merrily till the hay was made.

After this he found himself as badly off as before; and being almost starved again, he laid himself down at the door of Mr. Fitzwarren, a rich merchant. Here he was soon seen by the cook-maid, who was an ill-tempered creature, and happened just then to be very busy preparing dinner for her master and mistress; so she called out to poor Dick: 'What business have you there, you lazy rogue? There is nothing else but beggars; if you do not take yourself away, we will see how you will like a sousing of some dish-water; I have some here hot enough to make you jump.'

Just at that time Mr. Fitzwarren himself came home to dinner; and when he saw a dirty ragged boy lying at the door, he said to him: 'Why do you lie there, my boy? You seem old enough to work; I am afraid you are inclined to be lazy.'

'No, indeed, sir,' said Dick to him, 'that is not the case, for I would work with all my heart, but I do not know anybody, and I believe I am very sick for the want of food.'

'Poor fellow, get up; let me see what ails you.'

Dick now tried to rise, but was obliged to lie down again, being too weak to stand, for he had not eaten any food for three days, and was no longer able to run about and beg a halfpenny of people in the street. So the kind merchant ordered him to be taken into the house, and have a good dinner given him, and be kept to do what work he was able to do for the cook.

Little Dick would have lived very happy in this good family if it had not been for the ill-natured cook. She used to say: 'You are under me, so look sharp; clean the spit and the dripping-pan, make the fires, wind up the jack, and do all the scullery work nimbly, or – ' and she would shake the ladle at him. Besides, she was so fond of basting, that when she had no meat to baste, she would baste poor Dick's head and shoulders with a broom, or anything else that happened to fill in her way. At last her ill-usage of him was told to Alice, Mr. Fitzwarren's daughter, who told the cook she should be turned away if she did not treat him more kindly.

The behaviour of the cook was now a little better; but besides this Dick had another hardship to get over. His bed stood in a garret, where there were so many holes in the floor and the walls that every night he was tormented with rats and mice. A gentleman having given Dick a penny for cleaning his shoes, he thought he would buy a cat with it. The next day he saw a girl with a cat, and asked her 'Will you let me have that cat for a penny?'

The girl said: 'Yes, that I will, master, though she is an excellent mouser.'

Dick hid his cat in the garret, and always took care to carry a part of his dinner to her; and in a short time he had no more trouble with the rats and mice, but slept quite sound.

Soon after this his master had a ship ready to sail; and as it was the custom that all his servants should have some chance for good fortune as well as himself, he called them all into the parlour and asked them what they would send out.

They all had something that they were willing to venture except poor Dick, who had neither money nor goods, and therefore could send nothing. For this reason he did not come into the parlour with the rest; but Miss Alice guessed what was the matter, and ordered him to be called in.

She then said: 'I will lay down some money for him.'

But her father told her; 'This will not do, for it must be something of his own.'

When poor Dick heard this, he said: 'I have nothing but a cat which I bought for a penny some time since off a little girl.'

'Fetch your cat then, my lad,' said Mr. Fitzwarren, 'and let her go.'

Dick went upstairs and brought down poor puss, with tears in his eyes, and gave her to the captain. 'For,' he said, 'I shall now be kept awake all night by the rats and mice.' All the company laughed at Dick's odd venture; and Miss Alice, who felt pity for him, gave him some money to buy another cat.

This, and many other marks of kindness shown him by Miss Alice, made the ill-tempered cook jealous of poor Dick, and she began to use him more cruelly than ever, and always made fun of him for sending his cat to sea. She asked him: 'Do you think your cat will sell for as much money as would buy a stick to beat you?'

At last poor Dick could not bear this usage any longer, and he thought he would run away from his place; so he packed up his few things, and started very early in the morning, on All-Hallows Day, the first of November. He walked as far as Holloway; and there sat down on a stone, which to this day is called 'Whittington's Stone', and began to think to himself which road he should take.

While he was thinking what he should do, the Bells of Bow Church, which at that time were only six, began to ring, and their sound seemed to say to him:

Turn again, Whittington,
Thrice Lord Mayor of London.'

'Lord Mayor of London!' said he to himself. 'Why, to be sure, I would put up with almost anything now, to be Lord Mayor of London, and ride in a fine coach, when I grow to be a man! Well, I will go back, and think nothing of the cuffing and scolding of the old cook, if I am to be Lord Mayor of London.'

Dick went back, and was lucky enough to get into the house, and set about his work, before the old cook came downstairs.

We must now follow Miss Puss to the coast of Africa. The ship with the cat on board, was a long time at sea; and was at last driven by the winds on a part of the coast of Barbary, where the only people were the Moors, unknown to the English. The people came in great numbers to see the sailors, because they were of a different colour to themselves, and treated them civilly; and, when they became better acquainted, were very eager to buy the fine things that the ship was loaded with.

When the captain saw this, he sent patterns of the best things he had to the king of the country, who was so much pleased with them, that he sent for the captain to come to the palace. Here they were placed, as it is the custom of the country, on rich carpets flowered with gold and silver. The king and queen were seated at the upper end of the room, and a number of dishes were brought in for dinner. They had not sat long, when a vast number of rats and mice rushed in, and devoured all the meat in an instant. The captain wondered at this, and asked if these vermin were not unpleasant.

'Oh yes,' said they, 'very offensive; and the king would give half his treasure to be freed of them, for they not only destroy his dinner, as you see, but they assault him in his chamber, and even in bed, and so that he is obliged to be watched while he is sleeping, for fear of this horde of rats and mice.'

The captain jumped for joy; he remembered poor Whittington and his cat, and told the king he had a creature on board the ship that would despatch all these vermin immediately.

The king jumped so high at the joy which the news gave him, that his turban dropped off his head. 'Bring this creature to me,' said he; 'vermin are dreadful in a court, and if she will perform what you say, I will load your ship with gold and jewels in exchange for her.'

The captain, who knew his business, took this opportunity to set forth the merits of Miss Puss. He told his majesty: 'It is not very convenient to part with her, as, when she is gone, the rats and mice may destroy the goods in the ship – but to oblige your majesty, I will fetch her.'

'Run, run!' said the queen; 'I am impatient to see the dear creature.'

Away went the captain to the ship, while another dinner was got ready. He put Puss under his arm, and arrived at the palace just in time to see the table full of rats. When the cat saw them, she did not wait for bidding, but jumped out of the captain's arms, and in a few minutes laid almost all the rats and mice dead at her feet. The rest of them in their fright scampered away to their holes.

The king was quite charmed to get rid of such plagues so easily, and the queen desired that the creature who had done them so great a kindness might be brought to her, that she might look at her.

Upon which the captain called: 'Pussy, pussy, pussy!' and she came to him. He then presented her to the queen, who started back, and was afraid to touch a creature who had made such a havoc among the rats and mice. However, when the captain stroked the cat and called: 'Pussy, pussy,' the queen also touched her and cried: 'Putty, putty,' for she had not learned English. He then put her on the queen's lap, where she played with her majesty's hand, and then purred herself to sleep.

The king, having seen the exploits of Miss Puss, and being informed that her kittens would stock the whole country, and keep it free from rats, bargained with the captain for the whole ship's cargo, and then gave him ten times as much for the cat as all the rest amounted to.

The captain then took leave of the royal party, and set sail with a fair wind for England, and after a happy voyage arrived safely in London.

One morning, early, Mr. Fitzwarren had just come to his counting-house and seated himself at the desk, to count over the cash, and settle the business for the day, when somebody came *tap*, *tap*, at the door. 'Who's there?' said Mr. Fitzwarren.

'A friend,' answered the other; 'I come to bring you good news of your ship *Unicorn*.' The merchant, bustled up in such a hurry that he forgot his gout, opened the door, and who should he see waiting but the captain and factor, with a cabinet of jewels, and a bill of lading; when he looked at this the merchant lifted up his eyes and thanked Heaven for sending him such a prosperous voyage.

They then told the story of the cat, and showed the rich present that the king and queen had sent for her to poor Dick.

Dick Whittington and his Cat *opposite*: Dick sat on a stone and began to think which road he should take. The Bells of Bow Church began to ring and their sound seemed to say to him, 'Turn again, Whittington, Thrice Lord Mayor of London.'

"Turn again,
Whittington."
Thrice honoured
Citizen."

"Sir Richard
        Whittington,
"Lord Mayor
        of London."

As soon as the merchant heard this, he called out to his servants:

'Go send him in, and tell him of his fame;
Pray call him Mr. Whittington by name.'

Mr. Fitzwarren now showed himself to be a good man; for when some of his servants said so great a treasure was too much for him, he answered: 'God forbid I should deprive him of the value of a single penny; it is his own, and he shall have it to a farthing.'

He then sent for Dick, who at that time was scouring pots for the cook, and was quite dirty. He would have excused himself from coming into the counting-house, saying, 'The room is swept, and my shoes are dirty and full of hob-nails.' But the merchant ordered him to come in.

Mr. Fitzwarren ordered a chair to be set for him, and so he began to think they were making game of him, at the same time said to them: 'Do not play tricks with a poor simple boy, but let me go down again, if you please, to my work.'

'Indeed, Mr. Whittington,' said the merchant, 'we are all quite in earnest with you, and I most heartily rejoice in the news that these gentlemen have brought you; for the captain has sold your cat to the King of Barbary, and brought you in return for her more riches than I possess in the whole world; and I wish you may long enjoy them!'

Mr. Fitzwarren then told the men to open the great treasure they had brought with them, and said: 'Mr. Whittington has

Dick Whittington and his Cat *opposite*: Dick eventually became Sherrif of London, thrice Lord Mayor and received the honour of knighthood from Henry V.

nothing to do but to put it in some place of safety.'

Poor Dick hardly knew how to behave himself for joy. He begged his master to take what part of it he pleased, since he owed it all to his kindness.

'No, no,' answered Mr. Fitzwarren, 'this is all your own; and I have no doubt but you will use it well.'

Dick next asked his mistress, and then Miss Alice, to accept a part of his good fortune; but they would not, and at the same time told him they felt great joy at his good success. But this poor fellow was too kind-hearted to keep it all to himself; so he made a present to the captain, the mate, and the rest of Mr. Fitzwarren's servants; and even to the ill-natured old cook.

After this Mr. Fitzwarren advised him to send for a proper tailor and get himself dressed like a gentleman; and told him he was welcome to live in his house till he could provide himself with a better.

When Whittington's face was washed, his hair curled, his hat cocked and he was dressed in a nice suit of clothes, he was as handsome and genteel as any young man who visited at Mr. Fitzwarren's; so that Miss Alice, who had once been so kind to him, and thought of him with pity, now looked upon him as fit to be her sweetheart; and the more so, no doubt, because Whittington was now always thinking what he could do to oblige her, and making her the prettiest presents that could be.

Mr. Fitzwarren soon saw their love for each other, and proposed to join them in marriage; and to this they both readily agreed. A day for the wedding was soon fixed. They were attended to church by the Lord Mayor, the court of aldermen, the sheriffs, and a great number of the richest merchants in London, whom they afterwards treated with a very rich feast.

History tells us that Mr. Whittington and his lady lived in great splendour, and were very happy. They had several children. He was Sheriff of London, thrice Lord Mayor and received the honour of knighthood by Henry V.

He entertained this king and his queen at dinner after his conquest of France so grandly, that the king said: 'Never had prince such a subject.' When Sir Richard heard this, he said: 'Never had subject such a prince.'

The figure of Sir Richard Whittington with his cat in his arms, carved in stone, was to be seen till the year 1780 over the archway of the old prison of Newgate, which he built for criminals.

Thumbelina

here was once a woman who wanted to have a tiny, little child, but she did not know where to get one. So one day she went to an old Witch and said to her: 'I should so much like to have a tiny, little child. Can you tell me where I can get one?'

'Oh, we have one just ready!' said the Witch. 'Here is a barleycorn for you. It's not the kind the farmer sows in his field or feeds the cocks and hens with, I can tell you. Put it in a flowerpot and then you will see something happen.'

'Oh, thank you,' said the woman and gave the Witch a shilling, for that was what it cost. Then she went home and planted the barleycorn. Immediately there grew out of it a large and beautiful flower, which looked like a tulip, but the petals were tightly closed as if it were still only a bud.

'What a beautiful flower!' exclaimed the woman, and she kissed the red and yellow petals. As she kissed them the flower burst open. It was a real tulip, such as one can see any day, but in the middle of the blossom, on the soft velvety petals, sat a tiny girl, trim and pretty. She was scarcely half a thumb in height so they called her Thumbelina.

An elegant polished walnut shell served Thumbelina as a cradle, the blue petals of a violet were her mattress and a rose leaf her coverlet. There she lay at night, but in the daytime she used to play about on the table. Here the woman had put a bowl, surrounded by a ring of flowers, with their stalks in water, in the middle of which floated a great tulip petal, and in this Thumbelina sat and sailed from one side of the bowl to the other, rowing herself with two white horsehairs for oars. It was such a pretty sight! She could sing, too, with a voice more soft and sweet than had ever been heard before.

One night, when she was lying in her pretty bed, an old toad crept in through a broken pane in the window. She was very ugly and clumsy, and she hopped on to the table where Thumbelina lay asleep under the red rose leaf.

'This would make a beautiful wife for my son,' said the toad, taking up the walnut shell, with Thumbelina inside, and hopped with it through the window into the garden.

There flowed a great wide stream, with slippery and marshy banks; here the toad lived with her son. Ugh, how ugly and clammy he was, just like his mother! 'Croak, croak, croak!' was all he could say when he saw the pretty little girl in the walnut shell.

'Don't talk so loud, or you'll wake her,' said the old toad. 'She might escape us even now. She is as light as a feather. We will put her at once on a broad water-lily leaf in the stream. That will be quite an island for her; she is so small and light. She can't run away from us there, while we are preparing the guest chamber under the marsh where she shall live.'

Outside in the brook grew many water lilies, with broad green leaves, which looked as if they were swimming about on the water. The leaf farthest away was the largest, and to this the old toad swam with Thumbelina in her walnut shell.

The tiny Thumbelina woke up very early in the morning, and when she saw where she was she began to cry bitterly. On every side of the great green leaf was water and, no matter how hard she tried, she could not get to the land.

The old toad was down under the marsh, decorating her room with rushes and yellow marigold leaves, to make it very grand for her new daughter-in-law. Then she swam out with her ugly son to the leaf where Thumbelina lay. She wanted to fetch the pretty cradle to put it into her room before Thumbelina herself came there. The old toad bowed low in the water before her, and said:

'Here is my son. You shall marry him and live in great magnificence down under the marsh.'

'Croak, croak, croak!' was all the son could say. Then they took the neat little cradle and swam away with it. Thumbelina sat alone on the great green leaf and wept, for she did not want to live with the toad or marry her ugly son.

The little fishes swimming about under the water had seen the toad quite plainly and heard what she had said. They put up their heads to see the little girl, and thought her so pretty they were very sorry she should go down with the ugly toad to live. No, that must not happen. They assembled in the water round the green stalk which supported the leaf on which she was sitting and nibbled the stem in two. Away floated the leaf down the stream, bearing Thumbelina far beyond the reach of the toad.

On she sailed past several towns, and the little birds sitting in the bushes saw her and sang, 'What a pretty little girl!' The leaf floated farther and farther away. Thus Thumbelina left her native land.

A beautiful little white butterfly fluttered above her and at last settled on the leaf. Thumbelina pleased him and she, too, was delighted. Now the toads could not reach her, and it was so beautiful where she was travelling. The sun shone on the water and made it sparkle like the brightest silver. She took off her sash and tied one end round the butterfly. The other end she fastened to the leaf so that it glided along with her faster than ever.

A great May beetle came flying past. He caught sight of Thumbelina and in a moment had put his legs round her slender waist and had flown off with her to a tree. The green leaf floated away down the stream and the butterfly with it, for he was fastened to the leaf and could not get loose. How terrified poor little Thumbelina was when the beetle flew off with her to the tree! And she was especially distressed for the beautiful white butterfly because she had tied him fast. If he could not get away he might starve to death. But the beetle did not trouble himself about that. He sat down with her on a large green leaf, gave her honey out of the flowers to eat and told her she was very pretty, although she wasn't in the least like a May beetle. Later on, all the other beetles who lived in the same tree came to pay calls. They examined Thumbelina closely, and remarked, 'Why, she has only two legs! How very miserable!'

'She has no feelers!' cried another.

'How ugly she is!' said all the lady beetles – and yet Thumbelina was really very pretty.

The beetle who had stolen her knew this very well. But when he heard all the ladies saying she was ugly, he began to think so too and would not keep her. She might go wherever she liked. So he flew down from the tree with her and put her on a daisy. There she sat and wept, because she was so ugly the May beetle would have nothing to do with her. Yet Thumbelina was the most beautiful creature imaginable, so soft and delicate, like the loveliest rose leaf. She was perfect.

The whole summer poor little Thumbelina lived alone in the great wood. She plaited a bed for herself of blades of grass and hung it up under a clover leaf so she was protected from the rain. She gathered honey from the flowers for food and drank the dew on the leaves every morning. Thus the summer and autumn passed, but then came winter – the long, cold winter. All the birds who had sung so sweetly about her had flown away. The trees shed their leaves, the flowers died. The great clover leaf under which she had lived curled up and nothing remained but the withered stalk. She was terribly cold, for her clothes were ragged and she herself was so small and thin. Poor little Thumbelina would surely be frozen to death. It began to snow, and every snow flake that fell on her was like a whole shovelful, for she was only an inch high. She wrapped herself up in a dead leaf, but it was torn in the middle and gave her no warmth. She was trembling with cold.

Just outside the wood where she was now living lay a great cornfield. The corn had been gone a long time. Only the dry, bare stubble was left standing in the frozen ground. This made a forest for her to wander about in. All at once she came across the door of a field mouse, who had a little hole under a corn-stalk. There the mouse lived warm and snug, with a storeroom full of corn, a splendid kitchen and dining room. Poor little Thumbelina went up to the door and begged for a little piece of barley, for she had not had anything to eat for two days.

'Poor little creature!' said the field mouse, for she was a kind-hearted old thing. 'Come into my warm room and have some dinner with me.' As Thumbelina pleased her, she said, 'As far as I am concerned you may spend the winter with me. You must keep my room clean and tidy and tell me stories, for I like that very much.'

And Thumbelina did all that the kind old field mouse asked and did it remarkably well too.

'Now I am expecting a visitor,' said the field mouse. 'My neighbour comes to call on me once a week. He is in better circumstances than I am, has great big rooms, and wears a fine black-velvet coat. If you could only marry him, you would be well provided for. But he is blind. You must tell him all the prettiest stories you know.'

But Thumbelina did not trouble her head about him, for he was only a mole. He came and paid them a visit in his black-velvet coat.

'He is so rich and accomplished,' the field mouse told her. 'His house is twenty times larger than mine. He possesses great knowledge, but he cannot bear the sun and the beautiful flowers, and speaks slightingly of them, for he has never seen them.'

Thumbelina had to sing to him, so she sang 'Ladybird, ladybird, fly away home!' and other songs so prettily that the mole fell in love with her.

He did not say anything. He was a very cautious man. A short time before he had dug a long passage through the ground from his own house to that of his neighbour. In this he gave the field mouse and Thumbelina permission to walk as often as they liked. But he begged them not to be afraid of the dead bird that lay in the passage. It was a real bird with beak and feathers and must have died a long time ago and now lay buried just where he had made his tunnel.

The mole took a piece of rotten wood in his mouth, for that

glows like fire in the dark, and went in front, lighting them through the long dark passage. When they came to the place where the dead bird lay, the mole put his broad nose against the ceiling and pushed a hole through so the daylight could shine down. In the middle of the path lay a dead swallow, his pretty wings pressed close to his sides, his claws and head drawn under his feathers; the poor bird had evidently died of cold. Thumbelina was very sorry, for she was fond of all little birds. They had sung and twittered so beautifully to her all through the summer.

But the mole kicked him with his bandy legs and said: 'Now he can't sing any more! It must be very miserable to be a little bird! I'm thankful that none of my little children are. Birds always starve in winter.'

'Yes, you speak like a sensible man,' said the field mouse. 'What has a bird, in spite of all his singing, in the wintertime? He must starve and freeze, and that must be very unpleasant for him, I must say!'

Thumbelina did not say anything. When the other two had passed on she bent down to the bird, brushed aside the feathers from his head, and kissed his closed eyes gently. 'Perhaps he sang to me in the summer,' she said. 'How much pleasure he did give me, dear little bird!'

The mole closed up the hole again which let in the light and then escorted the ladies home. But Thumbelina could not sleep that night. She got out of bed and plaited a big blanket of straw and carried it off and spread it over the dead bird. She piled upon it thistledown as soft as cotton wool, which she had found in the field-mouse's room, so that the poor little thing should lie warmly buried.

'Farewell, pretty little bird!' she said. 'Farewell, and thank you for your beautiful songs in the summer, when the trees were green and the sun shone down warmly on us!' Then she laid her head against the bird's heart. But the bird was not dead. He had been frozen, but now that she had warmed him, he was coming to life again.

In autumn the swallows fly away to foreign lands. But there are some who are late in starting and then they get so cold that they drop down as if dead and the snow comes and covers them over.

Thumbelina trembled, she was so frightened. The bird was very large in comparison with herself – only an inch high. But she took courage, piled up the down more closely over the poor swallow, fetched her own coverlet and laid it over his head.

Next night she crept out again to him. There he was alive, but very weak. He could only open his eyes for a moment and look at Thumbelina, who was standing in front of him with a piece of rotten wood in her hand, for she had no other lantern.

'Thank you, pretty little child!' said the swallow to her. 'I am so beautifully warm! Soon I shall regain my strength, and then I shall be able to fly out again into the warm sunshine.'

'Oh,' she said, 'it is very cold outside. It is snowing and freezing! Stay in your warm bed. I will take care of you!'

Then she brought him water in a petal, which he drank. He told her how he had torn one of his wings on a bramble so he could not keep up with the other swallows, who had flown far away to warmer lands. So at last he had dropped down exhausted, and then he could remember no more. The whole winter he remained down there, and Thumbelina looked after him and nursed him tenderly. Neither the mole nor the field mouse learned anything of this, for they could not bear the poor swallow.

When the spring came, and the sun warmed the earth again, the swallow said farewell to Thumbelina, who opened for him the hole in the roof the mole had made. The sun shone brightly down upon her and the swallow asked her if she would go with him. She could sit upon his back.

Thumbelina wanted very much to fly far away into the green wood, but she knew that the old field mouse would be sad if she ran away. 'No, I mustn't come!' she said.

'Farewell, dear good little girl!' said the swallow, and flew off into the sunshine. Thumbelina gazed after him with tears in her eyes, for she was very fond of the swallow. 'Tweet, tweet!' sang the bird, and flew into the green wood.

Thumbelina was very unhappy. She was not allowed to go out into the warm sunshine. The corn which had been sowed in the field over the field-mouse's home grew up high into the air and made a thick forest for the poor little girl, who was only an inch high.

'Now you are to be a bride, Thumbelina,' said the field mouse, 'for our neighbour has proposed for you. What a piece of fortune for a poor child like you! Now you must set to work at your linen for your dowry, for nothing must be lacking if you are to become the wife of our neighbour, the mole!'

Thumbelina had to spin all day long, and every evening the mole visited her and told her that when the summer was over the sun would not shine so hot. Now it was burning the earth as hard as a stone. Yes, when the summer had passed, they would have the wedding.

But she was not at all pleased about it, for she did not like the stupid mole. Every morning when the sun was rising, and every evening when it was setting, she would steal out of the house door, and when the breeze parted the ears of corn so that she could see the blue sky through them, she thought how bright and beautiful it must be outside and longed to see her dear swallow again. But he never came. No doubt he had flown far away into the great green wood.

By the autumn Thumbelina had finished the dowry.

'In four weeks you will be married,' said the field mouse. 'Don't be obstinate, or I shall bite you with my sharp white teeth! You will get a fine husband. The king himself has not such a velvet coat. His storeroom and cellar are full, and you should be thankful for that.'

Well, the wedding day arrived. The mole had come to fetch Thumbelina to live with him deep down under the ground, never to come out into the warm sun again, for that was what he didn't like. The poor little girl was very sad, for now she must say good-bye to the beautiful sun.

'Farewell, bright sun!' she cried, stretching out her arms toward it and taking another step outside the house. Now the corn had been reaped, and only the dry stubble was left standing. 'Farewell, farewell!' she said, and put her arms round a little red flower that grew here. 'Give my love to the dear swallow when you see him!'

'Tweet, tweet!' sounded in her ear all at once. She looked up. There was the swallow flying past! As soon as he saw Thumbelina, he was very glad.

She told him how unwilling she was to marry the ugly mole, as then she had to live underground where the sun never shone, and she could not help bursting into tears.

'The cold winter is coming now,' said the swallow. 'I must fly away to warmer lands. Will you come with me? You can sit on my back, and we will fly far away from the ugly mole and his dark house, over the mountains to the warm countries. There the sun shines more brightly than here. There it is always summer and there are always beautiful flowers. Do come with me, dear little Thumbelina, who saved my life when I lay frozen in the dark tunnel!'

'Yes I will go with you,' said Thumbelina, and climbed on the swallow's back, with her feet on one of his outstretched wings. Up into the air he flew, over woods and seas, over the great mountains where the snow is always lying. If she was cold she crept under his warm feathers, only keeping her little head out to admire all the beautiful things in the world beneath. At last they came to warm lands. There the sun was brighter, the sky seemed twice as high, and in the hedges hung the finest green and purple grapes. In the woods grew oranges and lemons. The air was scented with myrtle and mint and on the roads were pretty little children running about and playing with great gorgeous butterflies. But the swallow flew on farther, and it became more and more beautiful. Under the most splendid green trees beside a blue lake stood a glittering white marble castle. Vines hung about the high pillars; there were many swallows' nests, and in one of these lived the swallow who was carrying Thumbelina.

'Here is my house!' said he. 'But it won't do for you to live with me. I am not tidy enough to please you. Find a home for yourself in one of the lovely flowers that grow down there. Now I will set you down and you can do whatever you like.'

'That will be splendid!' said she, clapping her little hands.

There lay a great white marble column which had fallen to the ground and broken into three pieces, but between these grew the most beautiful white flowers. The swallow flew down with Thumbelina and set her upon one of the broad leaves. There, to her astonishment, she found a tiny little man sitting in the middle of the flower, as white and transparent as if he were made of glass. He had the prettiest golden crown on his head and the most beautiful wings on his shoulders. He himself was no bigger than Thumbelina. He was the spirit of the flower. In each blossom there dwelt a tiny man or woman. But this one was king over the others.

'How handsome he is!' whispered Thumbelina to the swallow.

The little king was very much frightened by the swallow, for in comparison with one as tiny as himself he seemed a giant. But when he saw Thumbelina, he was delighted, for she was the most beautiful girl he had ever seen. So he took his golden crown off his head and put it on hers, asking her her name and if she would be his wife, and then she would be queen of all the flowers. Yes, he was a different kind of husband from the son of the toad and the mole with the black-velvet coat. So she said yes to the king. And out of each flower came a lady and gentleman, each so tiny and pretty that it was a pleasure to see them. Each brought Thumbelina a present, but the best of all was a beautiful pair of wings which they fastened on her back, and now she too could fly from flower to flower. They all wished her joy, and the swallow sat above in his nest and sang the wedding march as well as he could. But he was sad, because he was very fond of Thumbelina and did not want to be separated from her.

'You shall not be called Thumbelina!' said the spirit of the flower. 'That is an ugly name, and you are much too pretty for that. We will call you May Blossom.'

'Farewell, farewell!' said the little swallow with a heavy heart and flew away to farther lands, far, far away, right back to Denmark. There he had a little nest above a window, where his wife lived, who can tell fairy stories. 'Tweet, tweet!' he sang to her. And that is the way we learned the whole story.

The Three Bears

nce upon a time there were Three Bears, who lived together in a house of their own, in a wood. One of them was a Little, Small Wee Bear; and one was a Middle-sized Bear, and the other was a Great, Huge Bear. They had each a pot for their porridge: a little pot for the Little, Small, Wee Bear; and a middle-sized pot for the Middle Bear: and a great pot for the Great, Huge Bear. And they had each a chair to sit in: a little chair for the Little, Small, Wee Bear; and a middle-sized chair for the Middle Bear; and a great chair for the Great, Huge Bear. And they had each a bed to sleep in: a little bed for the Little, Small, Wee Bear; and a middle-sized bed for the Middle Bear; and a great bed for the Great, Huge Bear.

One day, after they had made the porridge for their breakfast, and poured it into their porridge-pots, they walked out into the wood while the porridge was cooling, that they might not burn their mouths, by beginning too soon to eat it. And while they were walking, a little girl called Goldilocks came to the house. She could not have been a very good little girl; for first she looked in at the window, and then she peeped in at the keyhole; and seeing nobody in the house, she lifted the latch. The door was not fastened, because the Bears were good Bears, who did nobody any harm, and never suspected that anybody would harm them. So Goldilocks opened the door, and went in; and well pleased she was when she saw the porridge on the table.

If she had been a good little girl, she would have waited till the Bears came home, and then, perhaps, they would have asked her to breakfast; for they were good Bears – a little rough or so, as the manner of Bears is, but for all that very good-natured and hospitable. But she was an impatient little girl, and set about helping herself.

So first she tasted the porridge of the Great, Huge Bear, and that was too hot for her; and she said a bad word about that. And then she tasted the porridge of the Middle Bear, and that was too cold for her; and she said a bad word about that too. And then she went to the porridge of the Little, Small, Wee Bear, and tasted that; and that was neither too hot, nor too cold, but just right; and she liked it so well that she ate it all up: but Goldilocks was annoyed with the little porridge-pot, because it did not hold enough for her.

Then Goldilocks sat down in the chair of the Great, Huge Bear, and that was too hard for her. And then she sat down in the chair of the Middle Bear, and that was too soft for her. And then she sat down in the chair of the Little, Small, Wee Bear, and that was neither too hard, nor too soft, but just right. So she seated herself in it, and there she sat till the bottom of the chair came out, and down she came, plump upon the ground. And Goldilocks was annoyed about that too.

Then Goldilocks went upstairs into the bed-chamber in which the Three Bears slept. And first she lay down upon the bed of the Great, Huge Bear; but that was too high at the head for her. And next she lay down upon the bed of the Middle Bear; and that was too high at the foot for her. And then she lay down upon the bed of the Little, Small, Wee Bear; and that was neither too high at the head, nor at the foot, but just right. She covered herself up comfortably, and lay there till she fell asleep.

By this time the Three Bears thought their porridge would be cool enough; so they came home. Now Goldilocks had left the spoon of the Great, Huge Bear, standing in his porridge.

'Somebody has been at my porridge!' said the Great Huge Bear, in his great, rough, gruff voice. And when the Middle Bear looked at his, he saw that the spoon was standing in it too. They were wooden spoons; if they had been silver ones, Goldilocks might have put them in her pocket.

'Somebody has been at my porridge!' said the Middle Bear in his middle voice.

Then the Little, Small, Wee Bear looked at his, and there was the spoon in the porridge-pot, but the porridge was all gone.

'Somebody has been at my porridge, and has eaten it all up!' said the Little Small, Wee Bear, in his little, small, wee voice.

Upon this the Three Bears, seeing that some one had entered their house, and eaten up the Little, Small, Wee Bear's breakfast began to look about them. Now Goldilocks had not put the hard cushion straight when she rose from the chair of the Great, Huge Bear.

'Somebody has been sitting in my chair!' said the Great, Huge Bear in his great, rough, gruff voice.

And Goldilocks had squished down the soft cushion of the Middle Bear.

'Somebody has been sitting in my chair!' said the middle bear in his middle voice.

And you know what Goldilocks had done to the third chair.

'Somebody has been sitting in my chair and has knocked the bottom out of it!' said the Little, Small, Wee Bear, in his little, small, wee voice.

Then the Three Bears thought it necessary that they should make further search; so they went upstairs into their bed-chamber. Now Goldilocks had pulled the pillow of the Great, Huge Bear, out of its place.

'Somebody has been lying in my bed!' said the Great, Huge Bear, in his great, rough, gruff voice.

And Goldilocks had pulled the bolster of the Middle Bear out of its place.

'Somebody has been lying in my bed!' said the Middle Bear, in his middle voice.

And when the Little Small, Wee Bear came to look at his bed, there was the bolster in its place; and the pillow in its place upon the bolster; and upon the pillow was Goldilocks' pretty little head.

'Somebody has been lying in my bed – and here she is!' said the Little, Small, Wee Bear, in his little, small, wee voice.

Goldilocks had heard in her sleep the great rough, gruff voice of the Great, Huge Bear; but she was so fast asleep that it was no more to her than the roaring of wind, or the rumbling of thunder. And she had heard the middle voice, of the Middle Bear, but it was only as if she had heard some one speaking in a dream. But when she heard the little, small, wee voice of the Little, Small, Wee Bear, it was so sharp, and so shrill, that it awakened her at once. Up she started; and when she saw the Three Bears on one side of the bed, she tumbled herself out at the other, and ran to the window. Now the window was open, because the Bears, like good, tidy Bears, as they were, always opened their bed-chamber window when they got up in the morning. Out Goldilocks jumped; and what happened to her, I cannot tell. But the Three Bears never saw her again.

Jack and the Beanstalk

here was once upon a time a poor widow who had an only son named Jack, and a cow named Milky-white. And all they had to live on was the milk the cow gave every morning which they carried to the market and sold. But one morning Milky-white gave no milk and they didn't know what to do.

'What shall we do, what shall we do?' said the widow, wringing her hands.

'Cheer up, mother, I'll go and get work somewhere,' said Jack.

'We've tried that before, and nobody would take you,' said his mother; 'we must sell Milky-white and with the money do something, perhaps open a shop.'

'All right, mother,' said Jack; 'it's market-day today, and I'll soon sell Milky-white, and then we'll see what we can do.'

So he took the cow's halter in his hand, and off he started. He hadn't gone far when he met a funny-looking old man who said to him: 'Good morning, Jack,'

'Good morning to you,' said Jack, and wondered how he knew his name.

'Well Jack, and where are you off to?' said the man.

'I'm going to market to sell our cow here.'

'Oh, you look the proper sort of chap to sell cows,' said the man; 'I wonder if you know how many beans make five.'

'Two in each hand and one in your mouth,' said Jack, as

sharp as a needle for he was a clever lad.

'Right you are,' said the man, 'and here they are the very beans themselves,' he went on, pulling out of his pocket a number of strange-looking beans. 'As you are so sharp,' said he, 'I don't mind doing a swop with you – your cow for these beans.'

'Aha!' said Jack; 'you would like that, wouldn't you?'

'Ah! you don't know what these beans are,' said the man; 'if you plant them overnight, by morning they grow right up to the sky.'

'Really?' said Jack; 'you don't say so.'

'Yes, that is so, and if it doesn't turn out to be true you can have your cow back.'

'Right,' said Jack, and handed him over Milky-white's halter and pocketed the beans.

Back home went Jack, and as he hadn't gone very far it wasn't dusk by the time he got to his door.

'What, back already, Jack?' said his mother; 'I see you haven't got Milky-white, so you've sold her. How much did you get for her?'

'You'll never guess, mother,' said Jack.

'No, you don't say so. Good boy! Five pounds, ten, fifteen, no, it can't be twenty.'

'I told you you couldn't guess. What do you say to these beans; they're magical, plant them over-night and – '

'What!' said Jack's mother. 'Have you been such a fool, such a dolt, such an idiot, as to give away my Milky-white, the best milker in the parish, and prime beef to boot, for a set of paltry beans. Take that! Take that! Take that! And as for your precious beans here they go out of the window. And now off to bed with you. Nothing shall you drink, and not a bit shall you swallow this very night.'

So Jack went upstairs to his little room in the attic, and sad and sorry he was, to be sure, as much for his mother's sake, as for the loss of his supper.

At last he dropped off to sleep.

When he woke up, the room looked so strange. The sun was shining into part of it, and yet all the rest was quite dark and shady. So Jack jumped up and dressed himself and went to the window. And what do you think he saw? Why, the beans his mother had thrown out of the window in the garden, had sprung up into a big beanstalk which went up and up and up till it reached the sky. So the man spoke truth after all.

The beanstalk grew up quite close past Jack's window, so all he had to do was to open it and take a jump on to the beanstalk which was made like a big plaited ladder. So Jack climbed and he climbed and he climbed and he climbed and he climbed and he climbed till at last he reached the sky. And when he got there he found a long broad road going as straight as a dart. So he walked along and he walked along and he walked along till he came to a great castle, and on the steps there was a great big tall woman.

'Good morning, ma'am,' said Jack, quite polite-like. 'Could you be so kind as to give me some breakfast.' For he hadn't had anything to eat, you know, the night before and was as hungry as a hunter.

'It's breakfast you want, is it?' said the great big tall woman. 'It's breakfast you'll be if you don't move off from here. My man is an ogre and there's nothing he likes better than boys broiled on toast. You'd better move on. He'll soon come.'

'Oh! please ma'am, do give me something te eat, ma'am. I've had nothing to eat since yesterday morning, really and truly, ma'am,' said Jack. 'I may as well be broiled, as die of hunger.'

Well, the ogre's wife wasn't such a bad sort, after all. So she took Jack into the kitchen, and gave him a hunk of bread and cheese and a jug of milk. But Jack hadn't half finished these when – *thump! thump! thump!* The whole castle began to tremble with the noise of someone coming.

'Goodness gracious me! It's my old man,' said the ogre's wife. 'What on earth shall I do? Here, come quick and jump in here.' And she bundled Jack into the oven just as the ogre came in.

He was a big one, to be sure. At his belt he had three calves strung up by the heels, and he unhooked them and threw them down on the table and said: 'Here, wife, broil me a couple of these for breakfast. Ah, what's this? I smell the blood of an Englishman.'

'Nonsense, dear,' said his wife, 'you're dreaming. Or perhaps you smell the scraps of that little boy you liked so much for yesterday's dinner. Here, you go and have a wash and tidy up, and by the time you come back your breakfast'll be ready for you.'

So the ogre went off, and Jack was just going to jump out of the oven and run off when the woman told him not to. 'Wait till he's asleep,' said she; 'he always has a snooze after breakfast.'

Well, the ogre had his breakfast, and after that he went to a big chest and took out of it a couple of bags of gold and sat down counting them till at last his head began to nod and he began to snore till the whole castle shook again.

Then Jack crept out on tiptoe from his oven, and as he was passing the ogre he took one of the bags of gold under his arm, and off he ran till he came to the beanstalk. He threw down the bag of gold which of course fell in to his mother's garden, and then he climbed down and climbed down till at last he got home and told his mother and showed her the gold and said: 'Well, mother, wasn't I right about the beans? They are really magical, you see.'

They lived on the bag of gold for some time, but at last they came to the end of it, so Jack made up his mind to try his luck once more up at the top of the beanstalk. So one fine morning he got up early, and got on to the beanstalk, and he climbed and he climbed and he climbed and he climbed and he climbed and he climbed till at last he got on the road again and came to the great castle he had been to before. There, sure enough, was the great big tall woman a-standing on the steps.

'Good morning, ma'am,' said Jack, as bold as brass. 'Could you be so good as to give me something to eat?'

'Go away, my boy,' said the big, tall woman, 'or else my man will eat you up for breakfast. But aren't you the youngster who came here once before? Do you know, that very day, my man missed one of his bags of gold.'

'That's very strange, ma'am' said Jack, 'I dare say I could tell you something about that, but I'm so hungry I can't speak till I've had something to eat.'

Well the big tall woman was so curious that she took him in and gave him something to eat. But he had scarcely begun munching it as slowly as he could when – *thump! thump! thump!* They heard the giant's footsteps, and his wife hid Jack away in the oven.

All happened as it did before. In came the ogre as he did before, said that he smelled the blood of a young man. But he had his breakfast, as usual, this time of three broiled oxen. Then he said: 'Wife, bring me the hen that lays the golden eggs.' So she brought it, and the ogre said: 'Lay,' and it laid an egg all of gold. And then the ogre began to nod his head, and to snore till the castle shook.

Then Jack crept out of the oven on tiptoe and caught hold of the golden hen, and was off before you could say 'Jack Robinson'.

But this time the hen gave a cackle which woke the ogre, and just as Jack got out of he house he heard him calling: 'Wife, wife, what have you done with my golden hen?'

And the wife said: 'Why, my dear?'

But that was all Jack heard, for he rushed off to the beanstalk and climbed down like a house on fire. And when he got home he showed his mother the wonderful hen and said 'Lay,' to it; and it laid a golden egg every time he said 'Lay.'

Well, Jack was not content, and it wasn't very long before he determined to have another try at his luck up there at the top of the beanstalk. So one fine morning, he got up early, and went on to the beanstalk, and he climbed and he climbed and he climbed and he climbed till he got to the top. But this time he knew better than to go straight to the ogre's castle. And when he got near it he waited behind a bush till he saw the ogre's wife come out with a pail to get some water, and then he crept into the house and got into a large copper pot. He hadn't been there long when he heard – *thump! thump! thump!* as before. In came the ogre and his wife.

'Fee-fi-fo-fum, I smell the blood of an Englishman,' cried out the ogre; 'I smell him, wife, I smell him.'

'Do you, my dearie?' says the ogre's wife. 'Then if it's that little rogue that stole your gold and the hen that laid the golden eggs he's sure to have got into the oven.' And they both rushed to the oven. But Jack wasn't there, luckily, and the ogre's wife said: 'There you are again with your fee-fi-fo-fum. Why of course it's the laddie you caught last night that I've broiled for your breakfast. How forgetful I am, and how careless you are not to tell the difference between a live one and a dead one.'

So the ogre sat down to the breakfast and ate it, but every now and then he would mutter: 'Well, I could have sworn – ' and he'd get up and search the larder and the cupboards, and everything, only luckily he didn't think of the big copper pot.

After breakfast was over, the ogre called out: 'Wife, wife, bring me my golden harp.' So she brought it and put it on the table before him. Then he said: 'Sing!' and the golden harp sang most beautifully. And it went on singing till the ogre fell asleep, and commenced to snore like thunder.

Then Jack lifted up the lid very quietly and got down like a mouse and crept on hands and knees till he got to the table. Then he stood up and caught hold of the golden harp and dashed with it towards the door.

But the harp called out quite loud: 'Master! Master!' and the ogre woke up just in time to see Jack running off with his harp.

Jack ran as fast as he could, and the ogre came rushing after, and would soon have caught him only Jack had a start and dodged him a bit and knew where he was going. When he got to the beanstalk the ogre was not more than twenty yards away when suddenly he saw Jack disappear, and when he got up to the end of the road he saw Jack underneath climbing down for dear life. Well, the ogre didn't like trusting himself to such a ladder, and he stood and waited, so Jack got another start.

But just then the harp cried out: 'Master! master!' and the ogre swung himself down on to the beanstalk which shook with his weight. Down climbed Jack, and after him climbed the ogre. By this time Jack had climbed down and climbed down and climbed down till he was very nearly home.

So he called out: 'Mother! mother! bring me an axe, bring me an axe.' And his mother came rushing out with the axe in her hand, but when she came to the beanstalk she stood stock still with fright for there she saw the ogre just coming down below the clouds.

But Jack jumped down and got hold of the axe and gave a chop at the beanstalk which cut it half in two. The ogre felt the beanstalk shake and quiver so he stopped to see what was the matter. Then Jack gave another chop with the axe, and the beanstalk was cut in two and began to topple over. Then the ogre fell down and broke his crown, and the beanstalk came toppling after.

Then Jack showed his mother his golden harp, and what with showing that and selling the golden eggs, Jack and his mother became very rich, and he married a great princess, and they lived happy ever after.

Jack and the Beanstalk *opposite*: So Jack climbed and he climbed and he climbed and he climbed and he climbed till at last he reached the sky.

Jack and the Beanstalk *page 170*: He walked along and he walked along and he walked along till he came to a great castle, and on the steps there was a great big tall woman.

Jack and the Beanstalk *page 171*: Jack caught hold of the golden harp, but the harp called out quite loud, 'Master! Master!' Jack ran as fast as he could, but the ogre came rushing after.

Jack climbs
the Beanstalk.

Jack arrives at the
Giant's Castle

Jack runs away with
the Golden Harp.

One of a series of fund-raising posters dating from the 1920s showing a children's ward at St Thomas's Hospital, London. The ward illustrated on the poster is decorated with fairy-tale and nursery-rhyme tile pictures. Fittingly, the Special Trustees of St. Thomas's Hospital have been committed to preserving this special part of Britain's heritage since the 1970s. It is believed that the first children's ward in the world to be decorated with tile pictures was Lilian Ward at St. Thomas's. When Lord Lister opened it in 1901 he called it 'the most beautiful children's ward that has ever existed.'

OYEZ·OYEZ·OYEZ
THE·FAIRY·TALES
ARE·NOW·CLOSED
LITTLE·BOYS·AND·GIRLS
MUST·NOT·READ·ANY·FURTHER·

List of Tile Pictures with Artists and Locations

M.E.T. = Margaret Thompson (at Doulton from *c*. 1889 to *c*. 1926)
W.R. = William Rowe (at Doulton from 1882 to 1939)
J.H.Mc. = John H. McLennan (at Doulton from 1879 to 1910)
Un. = Unknown

Jacket: *The Sleeping Beauty*. Artist: M.E.T. The Royal Victoria Infirmary, Newcastle-upon-Tyne.
Frontispiece: *Little Red Riding-Hood*. Artist: M.E.T.
Wellington Hospital, Wellington, New Zealand.
Page 7: *The Babes in the Wood*. Artists: W.R. and J.H.Mc.
St. Thomas' Hospital, London.
Pages 8-9: *The Sleeping Beauty*. Artist: M.E.T. Private Collection.
Page 10: *Little Red Riding-Hood*. Artist: M.E.T.
Wellington Hospital, Wellington, New Zealand.
Page 15: *Cinderella*. Artist: M.E.T.
Wellington Hospital, Wellington, New Zealand.
Page 16: *Cinderella*. Artist: Un.
St. Thomas' Hospital, London.
Page 33: *Puss in Boots*. Artist: M.E.T.
Wellington Hospital, Wellington, New Zealand.
Page 34: Puss in Boots. Artist: M.E.T.
Wellington Hospital, Wellington, New Zealand.
Page 43: *The Sleeping Beauty*. Artist. Un.
St. Thomas' Hospital, London.
Page 44: *The Sleeping Beauty*. Artist: Un.
St. Thomas' Hospital, London.
Page 65: *Hansel and Gretel*. Artist: M.E.T.
Wellington Hospital, Wellington, New Zealand.

Pages 66, 67, 68: *Little Red Riding Hood*. Artist: Un. St. Thomas' Hospital, London.
Page 73: *Little Red Riding-Hood*. Artist: *Un*.
St. Thomas' Hospital, London.
Page 74: *Little Red Riding-Hood*. Artist: Un.
St. Thomas' Hospital, London.
Page 83: *The Golden Goose*. Artist: Un.
Made by W.B. Simpson & Sons.
Torquay Hospital, Torquay, Devon.
Page 84: *Cinderella*. Artist: Un.
The Royal Victoria Infirmary, Newcastle-upon-Tyne.
Pages 101, 102 *Cinderella*. Artist: Un.
The Royal Victoria Infirmary, Newcastle-upon-Tyne.
Page 111: *Little Goody Two-Shoes*. Artist: Un.
Made by W.B. Simpson & Sons.
Torquay Hospital, Torquay, Devon.
Page 112: *The Babes in the Wood*. Artist: Un.
Made by W. B. Simpson & Sons.
Torquay Hospital, Torquay, Devon.
Page 129: *Jack the Giant-Killer*. Artist: Un.
St. Thomas' Hospital, London.
Pages 130, 139, 140: *Dick Whittington* Artist: Un. St. Thomas' Hospital, London.
Pages 169, 170, 171: *Jack and the Beanstalk*. Artist: Un.
St. Thomas' Hospital, London.

Sources of the Fairy Tales

The stories are based on the following sources: *The Allies Fairy Book*, Edmund Gosse (ed.), William Heinemann, 1916: 'The Sleeping Beauty'. *Anderson's Tales*, Ward Lock, 1909: 'The Tinder Box'. *The Arthur Rackham Fairy Book* by Arthur Rackham, George C. Harrap, London, 1933: 'Puss in Boots', 'Hansel and Gretel'. *The Children's Encylopaedia*, Vol. III, The Educational Book Company Limited, London: 'The Babes in the Wood'. *Edmund Dulac's Picture Book for the French Red Cross*, Hodder and Stoughton, 1915: 'The Princess and the Pea', 'Cinderella'. *English Fairy Tales*, collected by Joseph Jacobs, David Nutt, 1890: 'Henny Penny', 'Whittington and His Cat', 'The Story of the Three Bears', 'Jack the Giant-Killer', 'Jack and the Beanstalk', 'The Story of the Three Little Pigs'. In addition, the drawing on page 174 is a detail from one by John D. Batten in this book. *Fairy Gold, A Book of Old English Fairy Tales*, chosen by Ernest Rhys, Dent, 1915: 'Little Red Riding-Hood'. *Goody Two-Shoes*, a Facsimile Reproduction of the edition of 1766, Griffin and Farrar, London, 1881: 'Little Goody Two-Shoes'. *Popular Stories*, collected by the Brothers Grimm, Oxford University Press, 1915: 'The Golden Goose'. *The Yellow Fairy Book*, translated by Andrew Lang, Longmans, Green and Company, 1894: 'Thumbelina'.

Publisher's Acknowledgements

The Publishers gratefully acknowledge the help and co-operation of Royal Doulton, who designed and manufactured most of the tiles illustrated in this book.

The Publishers would like to thank Louise Irvine for her help, and John Greene of the Tiles and Architectural Ceramics Society for his assistance.

The Publishers gratefully acknowledge the following for the valuable assistance given in obtaining photographs of the tile sets: Miss Mowbray and The Special Trustees and staff of St. Thomas' Hospital, London; The Royal Victoria Infirmary, Newcastle-upon-Tyne; Bill Black, ex-Publications Officer with the Wellington Hospital Board and the staff of the children's ward, The Wellington Hospital, Wellington, New Zealand; Torquay Hospital and the Torquay District Health Authority, Torquay, Devon; and Jocelyn Lukins, London.

Illustration Acknowledgements

Newnes Books, Feltham, Middlesex – André Goulancourt: Front jacket, pages 7, 16, 43, 44, 66, 67, 68, 73, 74, 83, 84, 101, 102, 111, 112, 129, 130, 139, 140, 169, 170, 171
Nova Pacifica Publishing Company, Wellington, New Zealand: Frontispiece, pages 10, 15, 33, 34, 65
Jocelyn Lukins, London: pages 8-9.